WHISPERING CHRISTMAS

A CANDLEWOOD FALLS NOVEL

STACEY WILK

≈

This book is dedicated to Jeannie Jones-Tatro.
For all that you do and all that you are.

PRAISE FOR STACEY WILK'S BOOKS

Through the Darkness "Wilk pens a heart gripping story that will leave you breathless." *Jen Talty, USA Today Bestselling Author*

The Essence of Whiskey and Tea: "If you enjoy a good series about family and love, then this novel is sure to soothe your soul." *Booktrib*

Time Won't Erase: "The power of redemption shines in this emotional story about second chances." *Caridad Pineiro, New York Times and USA Today Bestselling Author*

Taking Root: "...multiple layers of entertainment." *InD'Tale Magazine*

Whispering Christmas: "She makes you feel deeply for each character as if you a part of the Candlewood Falls family." *Mint Copy Services*

Defining Chances: The author masterfully weaves together real-life situations, creating a narrative that's both thought-provoking and emotionally resonant. You'll find yourself rooting for Ember and Raf as they navigate their troubled pasts and learn to let go of guilt and anger.
Hidden Gems Reviews

HAVE WE GOT A STORY FOR YOU!

Dear Readers:

Welcome to Candlewood Falls!

Each Candlewood Falls story stands alone. However, the end of one story doesn't mean the end of your favorite characters. They can show up in any Candlewood Falls book at any time.

Candlewood Falls is a unique world of connected stories by different authors whose characters, business, and events appear in each others' stories.

Think of Candlewood Falls as a literary soap opera.

Be sure to check out the Ready for Another Trip to Candlewood Falls page at the end to discover which other books include your favorite characters.

Happy reading!

Stacey Wilk, K.M Fawcett, & Jen Talty

PROLOGUE

Fire burst from the first-floor window. Yellow and orange flames, growing in the November wind, reached for the night sky. Smoke billowed and scented the air with an acrid perfume. Bystanders stood on Houston Hill Road in their pajamas, winter coats, and boots, gaping at the newly renovated Pink Diamond Hotel, all thinking how it could be their house instead and silently thanking God it wasn't. No one wished harm on the hotel or its owners, but a fire in the middle of the night had a way of reminding people how easily life could implode.

The owners stood together with their arms around each other as their aspirations took an elbow to the jaw. The smoke detector had sounded while they lay asleep in each other's arms on the third floor in the new owner's suite. Jumping from their deep sleeps, a fog hanging over their brains as if a cold front had swept through their warm dreams, the two owners shoved their feet into shoes, tripped over laces, and ran.

A fire shot from the back of the new, modern oven that had recently replaced the old relic that had been in the kitchen for seventy years. The owners didn't waste time trying to find the fire extinguisher that had been moved by the careless cabinet installer during his beer-ladened afternoon. What was a few beers on the job? He could still swing a hammer. They wouldn't have been able to find it anyway. Instead, they ran out the front door and called the fire department.

In a sleepy town like Candlewood Falls, the fire department was made up mostly of volunteers who startled at their scanners breaking into the silent night. Men and women donned their gear, grabbed their keys, and hurried to help a pillar of the community and his new girlfriend.

"Don't worry, Sticks," the tall man with broad shoulders and eyes the color of a crystal lake whispered into her ear. He always used the nickname he gave her when he wanted to lighten a mood. "I'll take care of this for you."

"Silas, we could lose everything." Tears brimmed her tired and unbelieving eyes. She wiped them away, hoping the man she loved wouldn't see. The fire would set them back. They had accomplished so much in little time. They had hopes and plans and they weren't getting any younger. Did she really want to start over *again*?

The Pink Diamond was due to open in time for the Candlewood Falls Christmas Showcase which, for the first time in a long time, was going to be held at the new hotel.

"We won't lose everything. We have what's important." He pulled her close. Silas was a man who needed little to be happy.

"Dad, are you and Claudia all right?" Silas' daughter, Brooklyn, pushed and shoved her way through the crowd that had grown.

No one asked how Brooklyn, who lived outside the center of town on the alpaca farm with her husband and child, already knew about the fire. She was too far away to see the flames or smell the smoke. Those two things weren't her clue. The second the call came in that Silas Wilde needed helped, most of the town jumped to action. A number of people dialed Brooklyn's house, to inform her, to give her a ride, or to offer a babysitter so she could get to her father.

Small towns were known for their tight communities and Candlewood Falls was no exception. The fire department fought the flames as if the Pink Diamond were their own. Residents with no experience hauled buckets and pointed garden hoses. Carter River, with his hair pointing north and his bathrobe flapping in the wind, shouted to hand him another bucket. Jameson Haffrey, who owned the garage in town, took the empty buckets back to the start of the assembly line. Axel Alvarez, the local artist still covered in paint because he wasn't asleep when his brother Raf, who worked for Silas, yelled into his phone that they needed to move their butts, had grabbed a garden hose from somewhere and pointed it at the converted mansion, but only managed to soak Pink Diamond's neighbor Van Wilde.

"We're fine." Silas wrapped his other arm around Brooklyn and kissed the top of her head.

"We can't have the showcase here." Claudia rested

3

her head on Silas' shoulder. She had forgotten to tell him she loved him before they went to bed. Her mind had been on the opening. If something had happened to him, she wouldn't ever forgive herself. She had never expected to find love later in life, but she had.

"No, I suppose we can't," Silas said. "Looks like Weezer gets her way after all."

Weezer River, the town's equivalent to Shirley MacLaine's sourpuss character in the beloved movie about friends in a similar style small town set in the deep south and Carter's wife, coveted the showcase. As Carter had run from their home to help his good friend, Weezer began making plans to hold the showcase once again at her winery.

Good thing everyone in town knew without hesitation that Weezer would not in her wildest dreams set fire to anything, let alone the home her friend Silas occupied.

Good thing, indeed.

CHAPTER ONE

Nyx Wilde paced her dressing room. The space was small and cramped with a makeup table, chair, and a couch built for two. The room smelled like lilies and hair spray. She could only take a few steps before turning around and going back the way she came. Not a big deal for someone whose legs weren't all that terribly long—but short legs or not, she needed to put miles under her feet.

Her suitcase was flung open on the stand. Tops, blouses, and kimonos spilled over the side of the suitcase in a tidal wave of colors and materials. She didn't care about the mess or about the ginger ale on the table that didn't help with the nausea but left a wet ring under the can that grew into a puddle and soaked the paperback book she read when she had five minutes.

All she cared about was the show before ten thousand people which was about to begin and her only good ear went in and out. The crowd's energy thumped against the walls, floor, and her chest. Her fans waited for Nyx to come on stage and give them the performance she always delivered and they had paid for. Only she couldn't.

The ringing in her right ear that was normally there had progressed to something resembling a motorcycle taking up residence in her head and distorting all other sounds. She prayed for it to stop, but it wouldn't this time.

The dressing room door flew open and banged against the wall. If she hadn't been facing that wall, she wasn't so sure she would've noticed.

Ten minutes ago, the motor roaring in her ear had stopped, but when she realized not only could she not hear the motor, but she couldn't hear anything—she panicked. The motor returned and thankfully, so did her messed-up hearing. She was glad to have her hearing, but not the everlasting tinnitus. She would not be able to sing tonight. There was no way.

"What are you doing in here? The band is waiting to go on." Miles stared at her with wide eyes and his top lip curled in a snarl, revealing that ugly, yellow canine tooth she hated but tried to overlook.

She didn't blame him for barging in angrier than a fox locked out of the henhouse. Miles was her manager and got paid very well to make sure this band and this tour ran like the well-oiled machine it was.

But he was also the man who had put the three-carat diamond on her left hand and right now she needed him to swap hats and understand she couldn't go on that stage if the devil himself appeared.

"I need a minute." If she could calm down, maybe the noise would go away. That's what the internet said to do.

Except her hands shook, and she couldn't take a deep breath to save her life. The room took the occasional spin around the block, making matters slightly worse.

"You don't have a minute. Do you hear that crowd?" He pointed behind him.

Not great, she wanted to say, but kept it to herself. As long as she faced him, she could hear him well enough and fill in the blanks by reading his lips. She was good at that, having had hearing problems since childhood.

"Give me a minute, Miles. I'm nauseous and don't want to throw up."

"Are you pregnant? Please tell me you're not pregnant. We have another eight months on this tour." He raked his hand through his blond hair. He might pull those plugs right out of his skull if he kept that up. He should try tugging on that yellow tooth instead. When had it begun bothering her so much?

Miles was a vain man in a business that made getting old hard. Too many male musicians who had entered the back nine of their lives dyed their hair or wore weaves or hats to hide the baldness. Miles worked out five days a week and expected everyone on the team to do it with him.

Climbing into her forties shouldn't matter, even with icons paving the way for her like Dolly Parton or Reba McIntyre, but age mattered and the perceptions of being whole mattered more. She would be seen as less than if word spread she couldn't hear right.

She stared at Miles. Disbelief shocked her senses. For the first time in years, she realized she didn't know this man. "What if I were pregnant? You wouldn't be happy about that?"

"Now is not the time to discuss this. You have to get on stage. There's a noise ordinance and we have to be done by eleven. If you don't get on now, you won't be able to play the entire set including the encore, and the fans will demand the encore."

"I can't get on stage." She had no choice but to be honest. He was right about what the fans would expect. If she couldn't deliver, then she would return their money or reschedule the show. Performers did that kind of thing all the time. Though she never had. Not in all the years she had toured the world. She could say she had a stomach virus. No one would argue with that. Or she could tell everyone she was pregnant just to freak out Miles, but then she'd have to explain to the press why there was no baby. And after tonight, there never would be either.

"Please stop playing games. We don't have time for this. Everyone is waiting for you."

"My tinnitus is so bad all I hear is a motor in my ear. The vertigo comes and goes. I can't sing tonight."

He turned away from her and threw his hands in the air. She had to turn him back around on the off chance he was speaking.

Miles looked at her with a softness in his eyes. Maybe he finally understood how hard this was for her and how scary.

He gripped her shoulders. "You have to go on, baby. We can't cancel now. Just push through, and you'll be fine. You know the music inside and out. Do your best. Tomorrow we hit the road, and you can rest. Okay?"

"Miles, it's bad this time. The worst it's ever been."

"You're going to be fine. You always are." He gave her shoulders a little squeeze.

"But this is different." She had pushed through in the past, but that was when the tinnitus was more of a constant hum. Those shows hadn't been great and some of the reviews had said as much, but the negative press had swept away like dirt under a new broom after her next album became available.

"You have to trust me. I would never do anything to hurt you. You can do it." He took her hand and led her down the hall.

She should object, but the fans needed her. They had spent good money to see her and Miles had only scheduled one night in this town. She couldn't let her fans down or Miles for that matter. Or the band. Her bandmates were like family to her.

With a deep breath and a kiss from Miles, she went on stage. She could do this. She was Nyx Wilde, girl from New Jersey who came to Nashville on a wing and a prayer, ready to prove the whole world wrong about her. She had created her dream career on her sweat equity. She would not allow a little thing like tinnitus to stop her.

The crowd's roar washed over her in waves. Her body pulsed as if every scream and holler electrified her nerve endings. Normally, she lit up when her fan's energy spanned the stadium, touching her. But the buzzing in her ear sent a sharp pain through her head. She wanted to duck against the noise, but forced herself to stand straight, arms high in the air. The lights blinded her. Her stomach turned in protest.

The first guitar note raged from the wall of amps. A

high-pitched agonizing screech echoed in her ear. The band began to play. The beautiful chords she had labored over and fell in love with now turned against her and tormented her. What was once her lifeline was now unendurable.

Her guitarist, Fletcher, stared at her with confusion crossing his face as his fingers danced over the fret. The crowd stopped screaming. The vibrations in her chest ceased.

"Nyx?" Fletcher mouthed.

She tried to look around, to make sense of what was happening, but her gaze fell to her red leather cowboy boots. She couldn't face anyone. The pain in her ears was too much.

Someone grabbed her arm, startling her. She stared into Miles' angry face. When had he come on stage? His mouth moved, but she did not hear him.

"What the fuck?" His lips formed.

She stole a quick glance at the audience. Wide eyes and gaping mouths stared back. She had no choice. She knew what she had to do and should have done it sooner.

She ran.

CHAPTER TWO

F ord McKay turned into his parents' driveway with enough force to scrape the bumper of his recently paid-off sedan. He cringed as the car bounced on its shocks, metal scraping pavers. If the bumper needed a paint job because of his haste to pick up his daughter, he would add the task to the endless list of things he needed to do but never seemed to get around to completing.

He parked behind his mother's white Audi, forced himself to avoid looking at the bumper, and headed for the front door. His parents' house stretched against the late November night sky. Landscape lighting accented all the best parts of the stucco house and the professionally landscaped flower beds lying dormant for the season.

Except for the small pine trees dressed in white lights and a red bow for each tree situated on either side of the double front doors. More lights flickered behind the frosted glass.

His mother had wasted no time bringing out the company who decorated homes for Christmas. Each year, Golda Ford McKay hired the professional light stringers and tree decorators to come out Thanksgiving weekend and turn their already picture-perfect home into a Christmas showpiece

White lights outlined the entire house, including the roof and the columns on the front porch. No colored lights for his mother. Everything had to be straight out of a Blossom Hill catalogue. The only reason Ford even knew what Blossom Hill was because his entire life his mother walked around with it under her arm from September until Thanksgiving.

He rang the bell.

Hurried footsteps echoed on the other side of the doors. His mother swung the door open with a martini glass half-full in her hand. "You're late."

"I'm aware."

"Well, come in. You're letting in all the cold air and my heat out." She turned and tapped away from him on her heels. She was still dressed for the day in her cream-colored tailored pants and matching cashmere sweater.

"Where's Delaney?" He unbuttoned his wool coat and followed his mother through the expansive hallway also decked out in the finest Christmas. A twenty-foot tree filled with gold and red glass ornaments snuggled into the space where the staircase met the wall. The banister was draped in lit greenery. Christmas music played quietly in the background.

In the kitchen, he tossed his coat over the stool at the island. Small under-cabinet accent lights cast a soft glow on the clean and mostly clutter-free quartz countertops. The chairs around the wood table were tucked in as if to guard said table.

"She's in the television room with your father. They're watching *Jeopardy*. Did you eat?" She opened the stainless steel refrigerator void of any fingerprints on its surface. The interior light tumbled into the dim room.

Living in a home that walked straight out of a magazine had been a difficult place to grow up in. He and his two sisters were taught at an early age that everything had a place and there was a place for everything. The McKays may have a staff to help clean, but the children of the household would do their parts.

"I'll get something to eat at home." He wasn't sure what was in the fridge at his place exactly. He usually did the grocery shopping on the weekends and it was only Wednesday. If he took a look in his mother's fridge, it would be stocked with all the things his father loved to eat and a few of the ones Ford and Delaney—especially Delaney—enjoyed as well.

"I still have leftovers from Thanksgiving. Why don't you take some? Then you and Delaney will have food for lunch and dinner tomorrow." She closed the door and leaned against the counter.

"It's fine, Mom. I've got it."

"I know you do, sweetie. A mother wants to feed her child no matter how old he becomes. Do you want a drink?" She held up her glass.

"I just want to grab Delaney and head home. It's been a long day." And still not near done. "Thank you for watching her."

"You know we love having her here. She's a bright spot with those cute bows she wears. She made one for your father to wear as a tie. She almost convinced him to put it on. I laughed for five minutes. In the bathroom, of course, where no one could hear me."

His father's sense of humor didn't often come out for a ride around the block. Wearing a child's attempt at making a clothing accessory best bought at Nordstrom was not in his dad's wheelhouse. Grant McKay loved his granddaughter, but he also loved the importance of appearances.

"He could amuse her and put it on while she's here, at least." His father was not one to play make believe. Delaney was obsessed with making bows out of duct tape in a world of colors and patterns. She loved to wear them to school—or anywhere. The bows were quirky and unusual—just like his beautiful and unique nine-year-old. If she wanted to look like a walking craft, so be it. He would not stop her from being who she was.

"You know your father. Humor is not his best trait. I wear the ones she makes for me."

"Thank you for that." Growing up, his parents did not embrace all his differences. He had wanted to follow a career in music. His father had put a stop to that as fast as putting out a fire. Grant claimed he would be a terrible parent encouraging his son to follow a road destined to poverty. He had also refused to pay for college.

"She likes them. They're harmless and adorable, actually. That's all that matters. You're doing a good thing for her, encouraging her."

"Like you encouraged me?" He shouldn't have gone there tonight.

"I'm human, Ford. Even I make mistakes. If I knew

then what I know now, I would be living a very different life."

"It's not too late." He never understood what his mother saw in his father except they came from the same circles and their families knew each other. Grant McKay was headed places. Was that enough? Maybe it had been.

"It is for me. Too set in my ways. But you still have time." She winked and drank her cocktail.

"For what? I'm too busy running a school and raising a daughter for much else." Even his love life suffered because of his schedule. Which was fine. There wasn't a woman in Candlewood Falls who had turned his head since his return four years ago.

"I see what your father and I did to you, being the only boy and the oldest. You carry the weight of the world on those shoulders of yours. Put the load down and let loose a little." She drained the rest of her drink.

"Are you suggesting I get drunk?" He dropped onto the stool.

"It wouldn't hurt, you know. Let Delaney spend the night. I'll get her to school and you go off and have yourself a real bender."

"I can't believe you're even joking about it." He wasn't completely opposed to the idea, but not on a school night when he had to be at work tomorrow bright and early to wrangle a high school full of students and half as many teachers who were ready for the holiday break and it wasn't quite December.

"I'm not condoning getting drunk. Not all the time anyway. When was the last time you did anything fun?"

If he thought about it long and hard, he would have

to say at least ten years ago. "I don't have time. I can't afford to slack off now that my application for superintendent is being reviewed." He wouldn't know whether or not he had the position until March, but he couldn't afford for anything to go wrong at school over the next four months. He had a plan for his career, and he would stick to it.

"Daddy." Delaney darted into the kitchen and threw herself into his arms.

The plastic bow knocked him in the chin, but he didn't care. She smelled like blueberry muffins and powder. He didn't know how much longer his daughter would want to hug him. He would take every opportunity thrown at him, literally.

"Hey, Lay-Lay. How was your day?"

Delaney slipped out of his embrace and straightened the red and green bow on her head. Delaney had already switched to her Christmas-themed bows, following quickly in her grandmother's footsteps with her love for all things Christmas.

"Dad, you have to stop calling me Lay-Lay. I'm not a baby."

Golda arched a brow and poured herself a large glass of water. Delaney still had a sweet roundness to her cheeks and a small nose. She also still sported a little of her baby belly too, making him think of those years when her baby thighs were full of adorable rolls and chubby fists that she would shake at him. He would blow raspberries into her belly and watch his infant squeal in delight.

"You may not be a baby, but you'll always be my

baby. Now, go grab your backpack and coat. We need to get home."

"Can I sign up for the Christmas Showcase this year?" Delaney remained planted in her spot, her wide gaze firmly on his.

"What do you want to do in the showcase?" Candlewood Falls held a Christmas showcase every year before the holiday. Almost everyone in town participated in short skits from singing to dancing to magic. He used to be a part of it as well until he went off to college.

"Sing."

"Sing?" He shot a look at his mother who only shrugged.

"I can sing, Daddy. Grandma says I'm a star. I want to do a Christmas song. I can make a new Christmas bow or maybe one that looks like Rudolph's ears. You have to sign me up. I have the flyer in my folder. Mrs. Schacter gave each of us one to take home."

"We'll see." He would have a word with his mother about encouraging his daughter to pursue singing. Delaney was not a great singer. Even though he wanted her to follow her heart and believe she could be anything, he didn't want her to get her feelings hurt or be embarrassed. She would be a far better set designer than a front person, singing lead. Father guilt, for thinking his daughter was incapable of singing, nearly killed him.

"Can I have your phone? I want to take a picture of Pop," Delaney said, yanking him out of his thoughts. She held out her hand.

"Why do you want to take a picture of Pop?"

"He agreed to wear the tie I made him for ten whole minutes. We're watching the clock on the cable box."

"He did, did he?"

"Your father is coming around?" Golda slipped out of her heels and sat opposite him. Fatigue weighed heavy on her lids.

His parents were getting older. He didn't always like that reminder. He wasn't ready for them to slow down. He wasn't ready for that to happen to him either.

"Make it quick." He surrendered the device. Delaney snatched it and ran from the room. He stood and shrugged back into his coat. "I should be able to pick her up after school tomorrow."

"Why don't you let me grab her. We can do a little Christmas shopping and you can go out. Maybe on a date."

"Please don't start. I'm not interested in any woman in Candlewood Falls. The good ones are already taken or they are parents of my students. Besides, I don't have the time for a relationship and it could confuse Delaney."

"Delaney understands more than you think. She would want you to be happy. As does your mother."

"I'm happy. See?" He forced a huge smile on his face, showing all his teeth like he used to do in school photos when he was about Delaney's age.

Delaney ran back into the room with her coat on and backpack secured in place. The bow was still present and accounted for. She wouldn't take it off until she hopped in the shower, and then she'd try to sleep with one. He stifled a chuckle. He had taken a ton of photos of her wearing those bows, so someday when she was an annoying teenager, he could use them to his advantage.

"Come give Lolli a big smooch and a hug." Golda stood and held her arms wide. Delaney hugged her grandmother, then they bumped hips as if dance music popped on. He did not recognize his mother when she acted this way.

"Let's go." He bit back the desire to use her nickname and waved her on instead. "See you soon, Mom. Say hi to Dad." He tried to not take notice his father hadn't bothered to come into the kitchen. He put a hand on Delaney's shoulder and led her toward the foyer, finally going home. He couldn't wait to get out of his suit and sink into his couch.

"Ford?"

"Yes?" He turned back.

"There's one more thing before you go."

"What's that?" Whatever she wanted him to do or see would have to wait. He could come back over the weekend.

"I wanted you to hear it from me first." She straightened her sweater that hadn't budged.

"Mom, can this wait?" As long as it had nothing to do with his parents' health, whatever town news she may have could wait. He received plenty of unwanted gossip all day long at school.

"I don't think so."

"Okay, if you insist. Let's have it." He waved a hand to beckon her on.

"Nicole Wilde came home."

A shock went through his system, but that happened every time he heard Nyx's name. The pain would pass, and he'd go on his way. "That's nice."

He would be sure to avoid the orchard and Main Street for a couple of weeks. She must be home in between shows. She did that from time to time.

"No, Ford. You don't understand. She's home for good. Her career is over."

The room tilted. *Home for good?* How could that be? A thousand questions jumbled in his mind, but he forced each one away. His mother might have the gossip wrong. Rumors had a way of taking on a life of their own. Nyx would not come back home permanently for any reason. She hated this small town with its tight grip, and she never got along with her father. Now that her mother had passed, she had less of reason to come back and stay. Visit one of her sisters, sure, but just for a visit. Candlewood Falls never fit Nyx with her grand ideas and wild dreams. He knew that better than anyone.

"What Nicole does is none of my business and has not been for a long time." He would take a quick look online about the career thing. He highly doubted Nyx would end her career. She was on top of the world.

He had looked a time or two or a hundred. He only wanted to know she was doing well. But he hadn't searched her in months. He had made a promise to himself that he would stop. Knowing about her usually ended with him feeling bad. Living in the past did him no good.

"I didn't want you to be surprised when you bump into her around town."

"Thank you for your concern, but I can't imagine why you'd think I care either way. Nicole and I are ancient history." They broke up more years ago than he wanted to count. They had stayed friends for a while, but that hadn't lasted either.

"Daddy, who is Nicole?" Delaney tugged on the arm of his coat.

"An old friend."

"She was more than that," Golda said, holding his gaze.

"Mom, that's enough."

"Well, she was."

"We have to go." He turned again, more than ready for this conversation to be over. He didn't know how he felt about Nyx being in town for good, but he wasn't about to dive into that either. He had a full life now. He wasn't that lovesick boy anymore. Nyx didn't matter to him in the same way.

"There's more."

"Mom, please. Why do you care so much about this?"

"She can't hear, Ford. She lost her hearing."

CHAPTER THREE

S omeone banged on the bedroom door. Nyx blinked open her eyes. When had she fallen asleep? The last time she had looked at her phone the time was around two in the morning. Now, the sun spilled around the shades' edges. The motorcycle in her ear still revved. She slammed the pillow over her head, wanting the noise in her ear and banging on the door to stop.

"Go away." She didn't care who was on the other side. Whoever it was could take a hike. She wasn't in the mood for visitors and in Candlewood Falls, almost anyone could have walked into her father's house and up the stairs. She wasn't entirely sure why she had even come back to her hometown. She hadn't been thinking straight. Truthfully, she hadn't been thinking at all.

After her embarrassing moment on stage, she had flown home to Tennessee, thrown things in a suitcase, called a real estate agent and booked a flight to New Jersey. Her phone and social media had blown up, but she ignored all of it. She could not explain the humiliation choking her like an anaconda to everyone who begged for an answer—deserved an answer—she couldn't give. The world of country music was over and staying was out of the question. Unless she could get her hearing back to the way it was.

She could not go back on stage and risk the embarrassment of failing in front of thousands of people. Especially not after Miles had sent her a text stating she had ruined everyone's career and she should officially call it quits so the band and the crew could find other employment. He claimed no one wanted to wait it out for her. She didn't blame them, they had lives, but it still stung. Miles had also mentioned the engagement was off. She had responded with two simple words.

"Nyx, open the damn door. I know you can hear me." The banging continued.

She tossed the blankets off, stumbled over her boots, and threw open the door. "Petra, that's not a nice thing to say to someone like me."

Her oldest sister followed her into the room. Petra was lyrical in her black sweater and matching leggings. Her dark hair parted in the middle and cascaded below her shoulders in soft waves. Her high cheekbones were accented with a bronzer—probably the one Nyx had sent her—and her gaze was warm, but her square jaw was set.

"You heard me, didn't you? It smells like sour meat in here." Petra tore open the curtains and blasted the room with light.

"Close those." She stumbled back into bed and threw the blankets over her head.

"This room is a mess." Petra tugged the blanket away, tearing it right off the bed.

"Why are you still here?" She turned her back. The move was childish, but when she was around Petra, Nyx not becoming the baby sister proved difficult.

Petra was always like a mother figure, taking on the responsible role the oldest child always seemed to crave. Nyx didn't understand why Petra always wanted to be that way, except that their mom had always told Petra to watch out for her younger sisters. Petra was good at following rules.

Petra gripped her shoulder and turned her so their gazes met. "How bad is it today?"

"Bad."

"The nausea?"

"Not now." Which was true, but a bout of vertigo could show up at any time.

"Good. But you can hear me."

"You sound like you're down a tunnel with a motor running. Happy now?" Her hearing had worsened over the last year. She had ignored the signs, hoping it would get better. She had even started wearing ear protection on stage and at practice. A little too little. A little too late. The tinnitus had worsened because her hearing had worsened.

"No, Nicole. I'm not happy that my sister is in pain. That's why I'm here, trying to get you out of bed. I want to take you to your doctor's appointment."

"Not necessary."

"Of course, it is. You shouldn't go alone. I made a list of questions to ask the doctor and put it on my phone."

Petra pulled out the phone from the back pocket of her leggings.

"Put your phone away." She sat up and crossed her legs, holding a pillow to her chest.

"You don't want to hear the list? I'm sorry. I should've thought of that. I can text it to you."

She held up a hand to stop her lovely sister from bothering. "I don't need the list. I went to the doctor yesterday."

"What?" Petra's perfectly manicured eyebrows shot up.

"That's usually my word." She tried to make light of the situation, but a heaviness still filled her chest. She spent a lot of time saying *what* because of words she had missed during conversations. Sometimes at the frustration of other people who became tired of repeating themselves. Miles came to mind as one of those people.

"I don't understand. You have a doctor's appointment with the specialist today. You told me, and I put it in my calendar immediately. Oh, no. Did I mark it down wrong?" Petra's finger flew across her phone's screen.

"Petra, stop. You don't have the wrong date. I told you the wrong time."

"I understand. It's okay. You've had a lot on your mind. I would have—"

"On purpose. I told you the wrong date on purpose. I wanted to go alone." She couldn't bear to have her sister sit there, asking questions and taking notes as if Nyx were a child. Petra wouldn't mean anything by it, and Nyx loved her for wanting to be the support person, but Nyx had to do that one by herself if only to save herself from some of the humiliation that came with losing her hearing.

Petra sank onto the corner of the bed. Her mouth was slack and her eyes narrowed. Before Nyx could say anything that might resemble an apology, Petra shook her head and straightened her shoulders.

"Okay, that's not a problem. What did the doctor say?"

"My hearing is going to get worse. I have to live with it. The usual stuff." She shrugged it off, hoping Petra wouldn't see through her.

"That's all he said? Live with it?" Petra stood again and fisted her hands on her hips. She was about to catapult into full-blown protective big sister mode. So much for shrugging anything off.

"Don't you have a café to run?" If she couldn't act as if her appointment was no big deal, maybe she could distract her sister instead. Petra's life included a café of her dreams and a handsome chef who won her heart. Nyx would rather hear about good things than talk about her problems.

She envied Petra's new life. Guilt tried to choke those thoughts from her. Petra deserved all the happiness in the world. But Nyx had a perfect life once, and she wanted it back. Was that too much to ask for?

"It's not more important than you. Give me the details from the appointment. Are you getting hearing aids, finally? Medications? What?"

"I don't want to talk about it now. It's exhausting to follow what you're saying. Let me go back to sleep." When she could sleep, it was the only place she could get relief from the motor in her head.

"No sleeping. It's midmorning and a beautiful crisp day. You need to get out of the house."

"Why won't you leave me alone?"

"Because you're my sister, I love you, and Dad called me. He's worried about you." Petra went around the room, gathering dishes and cups and putting them by the door.

"Dad? Since when?" She was surprised he noticed that she hadn't come out of her room since her return. What he probably noticed was the rapid rate his dishes disappeared. She hadn't brought any of them back down to wash.

She and her father never got along. Growing up, her father was cold and distant. He went to work and forgot he had three daughters who needed him. He opposed every choice she had made. For spite, she did most of them anyway, which had led to a dream come true career that was now gone.

"You're going to have to work out your junk with him. He's different since Mom got sick."

"I really don't need you coming over here, telling me to get out of bed, that my room is a mess, and that I have to work out my stuff with Huck. Go away." She didn't want to consider that her father had softened in his later years because that would make her take a hard look at herself. Petra and their sister Ember had made new paths with their dad. She should be able to as well, but she couldn't.

"Get dressed. I want to take you out to lunch," Petra said, ignoring Nyx's plea that she leave.

"Hell, no. Everyone will see me and come asking questions."

"You need to get out of this room. Come to the café. Mav is making us a special lunch. We can eat in the kitchen so none of the customers will see us. You have to get back to the living."

"My life is over. Everything is ruined." Even to her she sounded like a petulant child.

"You don't have to fix anything today except take a shower and scrape some of that smell off you. Whether you like it or not, I'm going to change those sheets. I don't care if you're still in the bed. The choice is yours. But if I were you, I'd take a shower and get some fresh air. Or I can call Dad and tell him to come home because you want to spend time with him."

"You would not."

"I would. You can't avoid him too. You're living in the same house with him."

"I avoided him for my first eighteen years. I think I can avoid him for a few months." She pulled on the collar of her shirt and took a whiff. Her eyes watered. Yeah, she needed a shower. She'd give Petra that much.

"You promise no one will know we're at the café if I go with you?" She would go only because Petra would not stop nagging her until she did, and Mav was a pretty incredible cook.

Navigating a noisy café would drive her mad, though. The tinnitus would worsen. But if they weren't there long and she didn't have to talk to anyone except Petra and Maverick, Nyx might be okay. She missed spending time with her sisters. Nyx could admit that.

"I promise. Except for Sue who works in the kitchen and of course, Mav."

"Fine. I'll go." She hopped off the bed and grabbed some clothes from her suitcase. She did want to see Petra's place that had been open for about a year.

"You won't regret it."

"I already do." She plopped a kiss on Petra's cheek and hurried to the bathroom. The motorcade in her ear rumbled right along with her.

She would eat lunch and come straight back. As long as no one noticed her, she could manage for an hour. But this was Candlewood Falls, and she was a Wilde. Someone was bound to notice her.

She'd wear a disguise, a big hat and a thick scarf around her neck and oversized sunglasses. She had those. It wasn't as if anyone expected her to show up in town. Sure, the tour being canceled had made all the news channels, but no one knew she was here except for her family. She had kept her whereabouts a secret — at least for the time being.

She tore off her smelly pajamas and turned the water up high. The bathroom filled with steam. The idea of going into town seemed possible and for the first time in days she was less overwhelmed.

If she bumped into a cousin, of which she had a few, or her Uncle Silas, that would be okay too. But not anyone else. She wasn't ready for all the questions because she didn't have answers.

She had a disease that someday would most likely steal all her hearing. She had no career and a stark realization that she had no friends. Not true friends, the ones who stuck around when the going went from tough to beyond tough. So, she wasn't ready to walk around

Candlewood Falls and have her past knock into her as another reminder of what she had left behind.

She had been the girl who got out and made it. She had had it all. Almost all, anyway. She had the fame, the fortune, opportunities galore. She had a family who loved her even if her father was an obstinate old fool. But she never had the real love of a good man. Miles had left her at her worst. Her past relationships had failed because they were built on the wrong things.

She stepped into the shower, let the hot water soothe her muscles, and fought the next thoughts floating in the steam. Ford McKay had been the real deal once and she had loved him with her young heart and soul. She had also run as far and as fast from him as her legs would carry her.

He had wanted a wife, mother for his children, and a house with a fence. That dream was too small for her back then. She would have been lost, trying to make his wants fit her, like trying to fit into one of his t-shirts after they'd made love out in the woods as teenagers do and that soft worn-in cotton that smelled of soap would come to her knees, swallowing her up.

Maybe he had been right about some of his ideas. Maybe if she had taken the time to find real love—or not lost his—and start a family, she wouldn't feel so alone now that she was more scared than she had believed possible.

Funny how she thought of Ford when life was hard. He always sprung up that way like day lilies after a good rain. He probably never thought of her at all. He might even have himself a good old laugh at her expense if he heard about her mishap on stage and a boatload of tour dates canceled right around the holidays. He might be looking to say he told her so.

He would have been right.

CHAPTER FOUR

I f Nyx tried to eat now, she would vomit. The salad placed before her was beautiful in its vibrant colors of greens, purples, and whites, but she couldn't swallow one bite. The motor in her right ear had revved to a new level, and she fought to focus on what Petra and Mav had said to her for the past hour.

They were not in the kitchen of the Creek and Crumb Café. Petra sat opposite her at a table tucked in the corner of the dining area. They had a view of the Candlewood Falls River and the outdoor tables set on a cobblestone patio from their spot. The sun bounced off the water that bordered Creek and Crumb's outdoor seating and decorated the dark water in sparks of white light. The café was adorable with its cream walls and big windows. The floors were wide wood planks that sloped because they were original to the building and Mav had insisted they retain as much of the old charm as possible. Leaving her and Petra to eat, he had returned to the kitchen to help his employees.

The background noise in the kitchen was worse than the dining space. Between the commands being shouted about grabbing hot food, or bursts of expletives, and the clanking of pots and utensils, Nyx's head hurt. The heat made her nauseous. She had asked to sit amongst the patrons where the conversations were muted, but in a corner table not visible from the door. She still wasn't ready to bump into a familiar face. If she were lucky, she could go the whole time in Candlewood Falls without seeing anyone she knew besides her family. The problem was she had no idea how long she'd be here.

While trying to have lunch, her phone had blown up with texts from Luther, her sound guy, wanting to know how she was and when she would be back to work. She put the phone on Do Not Disturb. She couldn't answer Luther's questions any more than she could answer the questions coming in from the industry's journalists. She had forwarded all the emails to her assistant, Mandy, and would be sending the texts next.

Mav waved Petra over from his spot near the pass-through window.

"I'll be right back. Will you be okay?" Petra slid from her seat.

"I'm fine. Take your time." Sitting alone for a few minutes would be a relief.

Mav put his hand on Petra's low back and leaned in to say something in her ear. From her vantage point, Nyx could read Mav's lips. *Thank you for last night.* Petra placed a hand on Mav's cheek and looked at her man with longing. Nyx turned away, embarrassed that she had stumbled upon such an intimate moment.

She hated to admit this to herself, and certainly

would not admit it to another living soul, but watching Petra and Mav longingly glance at each other or laugh in that inside joke kind of way turned her stomach almost as much as the heat in the kitchen. Nyx was so happy for her sister and incredibly envious at the same time. The joy of seeing her sister succeed and the pain of Nyx's life crumbling in such a fantastic way were two sides of the same unwanted coin, spinning her into a horrible person.

All that jealousy stole her breath. She needed air and pushed out the glass doors into the crisp afternoon that smelled like seaweed and woodsmoke. The walking bridge was dressed for Christmas with full-size nutcrackers along the way. Nyx hurried down the path toward Main Street.

The sidewalk was mostly empty this time of day, and Nyx was grateful. Her car—well, her mother's old car— was back at her father's house. She would either have to walk, which would take close to an hour because everything in Candlewood Falls was spread out, or she could head over to the orchard, maybe catch a ride from one of her cousins. She couldn't go back into the café now that she had made a fool of herself, running for the hills. She should have stayed in bed.

Her phone vibrated in her pocket. She wanted to ignore it, but the interruption was probably Petra because only her sisters could bypass the Do Not Disturb feature. If Nyx didn't answer, Petra would send the Wilde family cavalry. Out of choices, Nyx read the screen. Petra had sent a text.

Where are you?
Needed air. Not feeling well. Sorry.
Where are you though?

Walking. I'll find a way home. Love you.

Are you sure? I can come get you.

No. Thanks for lunch. Nyx put her phone back in her pocket. She would walk home. The time and the fresh air would do her some good and maybe diminish the pathetic feelings of sadness and loss.

The Green Bean came into view. She always loved their coffee. On any other trip, she would go right in and order a large with skim milk, but not today. Everyone in town stopped in there sometime during their travels. And with the holiday shoppers about, she was bound to see someone she knew.

Uncle Silas' new boutique hotel was just around the corner from the coffee shop. Petra had told her about the fire that delayed the opening and changed the venue for the annual Christmas Showcase. Nyx had performed in that showcase every year from the age of nine to eighteen before she ran off to Nashville and the life of her dreams.

Curiosity had the best of her. She wanted to see the old renovated mansion that used to belong to Georgette Hill, the cranky eccentric old lady. Mrs. Hill had willed her place to Uncle Silas and his girlfriend Claudia. Boy, was that a crazy story.

Nyx loved her uncle. Seeing him might hit the spot. He was certainly the family's most unique relative. He might understand what she was going through because he never fit in to society in the typical way. She didn't any longer but couldn't come to terms with it. She didn't want to give up on the possibility that something might make the tinnitus stop.

She had been to several of the best doctors and no one had the answer she wanted. She would not accept that her future would consist of wearing hearing aids to help the tinnitus recede and to make hearing simple conversation possible. There had to be a better way. She had found some holistic techniques she could still try. Maybe they would be her way out.

A woman came out of the Green Bean with a little girl wearing a red and green plastic Christmas bow on her head. Neither was familiar to her. Nyx smiled at them both and turned up Houston Hill Road, looking forward to seeing her uncle.

"Nicole? Nicole Wilde, is that you?"

The words drifted toward her down a long tunnel, much like she had heard Petra all day. She could pretend she didn't hear this woman calling out to her. Ignoring this person would be simple enough and extremely easy to explain, if the need arose. The people who weren't angry at her for leaving music were often the ones who pitied her.

But her mother's teachings floated up in her head— never be rude. She missed her mother so much her heart ached. Nyx didn't want to let Ruby down, more so because she was gone, so she stopped to face the woman and the little girl.

"Hello. Yes, I'm Nicole. It's nice to see you again." She rarely used her given name. Only people she grew up around would refer to her that way.

She truly could not place the woman, but she didn't remember everyone in Candlewood Falls. This could be the mother of a friend from elementary school. The woman was probably around her parents' age, very well put together in her black wool coat and plaid scarf. If the designer bag hanging off the lady's arm was real, it cost a small fortune, as did those gold earrings.

Nyx wanted this person to feel as if she remembered her, especially if this woman was a fan. Nyx had learned that trick on the road. She wished the tinnitus would quit so it wasn't difficult to focus.

"Lolli, you know her?" The little girl stared up at the glamorous woman in amazement.

"I used to when she was much younger." This Lolli person turned to her. "You don't remember me, do you?"

Nyx racked her brain. Maybe this was a friend of her mother's. "You knew my mother, Ruby."

"I did. But that wasn't it." Lolli's smile spread wide and with ease.

"I love your music," the little girl said. "My name is Delaney." Delaney stuck out her hand.

Nyx bit back a chuckle. Delaney was adorable with her curly brown hair and big green eyes. "It's nice to meet you, Delaney. I love your bow." She made sure to give Delaney a solid handshake.

Delaney's face lit up like twinkle lights. "Thank you. I made it myself."

"That's very impressive. I'm so glad you're a fan. I don't have a lot of fans your age. Did your... Lolli play my music for you?" It took her a second to remember the unusual, but also adorable, name for what must be Delaney's grandmother.

"No, my dad is huge fan. He has all your albums."

"How nice. Who's your dad? Maybe I went to high school with him."

"Me."

Ford forced his knees to lock because if he didn't, he would fall on his ass. The world shifted under him when his gaze landed on Nyx speaking with Delaney. His instincts yelled to run in the other direction, get as far away from her as possible. He would have if he wasn't the father of the child in conversation with his old girl-friend and the fact he was the high school principal and had a reputation to uphold.

Nyx squared her shoulders and held his gaze with that fiery blue one of hers. "Hello, Ford." She turned to his mother. "Mrs. McKay, I didn't realize it was you. I'm sorry about that. I should have. Not sure what got into me." Nyx leaned closer to his mother.

She was focusing. He still remembered that she would do that on the days that her hearing was a bother. When they were young, it was only her one ear that didn't always work right. Nyx, or better yet his Nicole, would lean in to make sure she didn't miss what someone would say.

"Not a problem, sweetheart. It's been many years. I'm a little older now."

"You still look fantastic." Nyx placed a hand on Mom's arm.

"Mom, don't you have that appointment to get to?" He tried to usher his mother to the car parked down the street, but she wouldn't budge.

"I canceled that appointment, Ford, dear," his mother said, still looking at Nyx.

"It was nice to see you, Nyx, but we have to go." If his mother wouldn't take the hint, then he would have to end the conversation himself. He had nothing to say to Nyx and he could guess she had very little to say to him too. They had parted ways so long ago, dating her seemed like a part of another lifetime.

"Dad, can I get her autograph?" Delaney tugged on his coat.

"No. Miss Nyx doesn't have time for that." If he had only stayed in Green Bean five more minutes, he might've missed this whole encounter. All he wanted to do was get off the sidewalk.

"Time for what?" Nyx asked, with confusion across her beautiful features and looking between him and Golda. Damn Nyx was still as gorgeous.

"Can I have your autograph?" Delaney produced a pen from her backpack.

"Of course." Nyx took the pen.

Nyx had misstepped. She had missed Delaney saying autograph. Her hearing was a big problem for her today. They all stood close enough that anyone with regular hearing would've picked up Delaney's question, but Nyx had missed half of it. He warned his heart not to go soft on him now.

"Make it quick," he said.

His mother shot him a death glare. He gave her one back. He did not care if he was being less than gracious to the great and powerful Nyx Wilde. He knew her intimately before she was anything except Nicole, daughter of that ornery Huck Wilde. She wasn't anyone special. Except she had been once—to him.

"How long will you be in town?" his mother said.

"I'm not sure."

"Can we give you a ride?" Again, his mother forced

the conversation. She had to know he didn't want to stand there talking with Nyx.

"No," he said at the same time Nyx said no, thank you.

"I'm going to walk over to my uncle's."

"Will you be performing in the Christmas Show-case?" Delaney said. "I want to, if my dad says it's okay."

"What will you be doing?" Nyx asked, giving Delaney her full attention.

He should have seen this coming. It had been a huge mistake to introduce Delaney to Nyx's music, but he couldn't stay away from it. She was a great talent. He had to give her that much. He had often wondered if any of those songs about heartbreak and the one that got away might be about him. Foolish. She had taken off so quickly and never wanted anything from him after that. He would be the last thing on her mind.

"I sing. Like you. I want to be a singer in a band someday."

Nyx stared at him but said nothing. She didn't have to say a word. He could practically read her mind. He had refused to go with her when she left town to pursue music. She had to wonder, how could he encourage his child to play in that sand box? He wasn't doing that. Not that one.

"Delaney could use a little practice," Golda said.

"Can't we all." Nyx laughed.

"Could you teach me? Maybe then my dad will say yes instead of telling me I'm not ready. He doesn't want me to sing until I've had more practice."

Golda arched a brow.

Heat filled his cheeks.

"I think that's a splendid idea. I'll pay you," his mother chimed in before he could scrape his jaw off the ground. Leave it to his child to throw him right under the bus.

"I couldn't," Nyx said.

"See? She can't." He held out a hand as if that gesture would explain Nyx's answer better than she had.

Nyx glared at him, but the look disappeared as quickly as it arrived. Her face was neutral as soon as he blinked.

"What are you doing while you're in town?" Golda said.

"I... I... don't have any concrete plans."

"Ford, dear, don't you think Delaney would benefit by Nyx's expertise?"

"Mrs. McKay, I don't think you understand—"

"Nicole, it's about time you called me Golda or Goldie. Leave the Mrs. McKay stuff behind."

"Okay, Golda, I don't think you understand. I don't give singing lessons. I'm working through some personal stuff and then heading back to the road."

"Oh, please." Delaney jumped up and down with her hands in prayer. "I could tell all the kids at school that my singing teacher is you. That would be the best. They don't all like me."

Nyx looked between him and his mother,

His mother mouthed *she doesn't have a lot of friends.* Delaney didn't hear Golda and Nyx could read her lips. His heart fell, landing in his shoes. His little girl struggled at school in the social arena. He didn't understand why. She was sweet and funny. Sure, she was quirky, but she needed to be her own person. He hoped it wasn't the bows, but it probably was because kids could be cruel when another was different.

Nyx worked her lip under her teeth. He needed to put a stop to this singing lesson business. He couldn't allow her to slip into his life that easily as if nothing had ever happened between them. It may have been a long time ago, but he had been hurt by this woman more than once.

"I'll help. If it's okay with you, Ford. But you can't pay me. That's my stipulation." Nyx held up her hand.

Golda glared at him again. Delaney looked up at him with tear-rimmed eyes. He wished the sidewalk would swallow him up. If he said no now, he would go down in history as the worst father and at the holidays.

He squatted down to meet Delaney's gaze. He took a deep breath. "Are you sure you want to be in the Christmas Showcase?"

"It's the only thing in the world I want to do. Please, Daddy. I'll do all my homework without you having to tell me. I'll keep my room clean. Please. Please. Please." She bounced on her toes.

Typical overreactive kid reaction. He could probably bargain that showcase away with promises of more duct tape for the bows or tickets to a Broadway show that were too expensive or any number of things he would otherwise say no to right now. But he slapped his mouth shut because as a single parent, he had to often come down on the side of disciplinarian. He had no one to pass off the responsibility to when days were tough. He had to live with saying no when he would love to say yes to his little girl who wouldn't stay little for long.

He would regret agreeing to Nyx being anything to

Delaney. Nyx as her teacher would mean he would have to see her. Regret wasn't for the future. He already did.

Standing, his knees popping and cracking, he faced Nyx. "You don't have to do this. I can find another teacher." He wanted her to say no and take him off the hook.

He didn't think Delaney was a good enough singer to perform. His heart broke because he truly wanted his little girl to be good at everything. Every parent should tell their kid that he or she could do anything they put their mind to, but that wasn't the truth. Knowing limitations was important.

He hated to admit that Delaney was better off with obtainable dreams because his own parents had told him that trying to be a paid musician was a worthless endeavor. At first, he had been crushed, but in time he saw he didn't have what it took. Nyx had the wild hair across her bottom that drove her to do things most normal people didn't. His parents had saved him a lot of disappointment.

As a man in academia, he witnessed too many far-fetched pursuits go up in smoke with nothing left behind except the tattered remains of a soul.

Music was not a practical career choice. He wanted Delaney to be able to take care of herself someday. It's one thing to encourage her to be her own person, but it's another to fill her with false hope.

Music wasn't going to provide her with a reliable income. Nyx was an outlier. Making albums, selling out stadiums, singing on movie soundtracks didn't happen for the millions of people who tried. If he encouraged Delaney to sing and perform, he would lead her right into a life full of disappointments. His job was to protect her.

Nyx glanced at Delaney who held her hands in prayer under her pudgy chin and looked up at Nyx through long lashes. His heart melted.

"I don't mind. But if it turns out I'm not the best teacher, I'll tell you, and you can find someone better suited," Nyx said to him.

"You're going to be a great teacher, dear." His mother gripped Nyx's shoulder and looked her square in the eye. He suspected Golda understood what was happening for Nyx right now. The news and social media had replayed the clip of her holding her head on stage and running off a trillion times. Anyone who followed music or Nyx would have seen her despair. But that didn't mean he had forgiven her for breaking his heart.

"Okay, you can have singing lessons once a week. That's it," he said to Delaney who threw herself into his arms.

If this woman whom he had once loved but broke his heart, even bruised his daughter's, he would not be held responsible for his actions.

"Wonderful. You can use my house. I pick Delaney up after school. Tomorrow?" Golda said.

"Tomorrow should work." Nyx worked her lip again.

"Then it's settled," Golda said. "Delaney, let's give Daddy and Miss Nyx a minute to square away the details. We'll meet you at the car."

When his mother and daughter were out of earshot, he turned to Nyx. "You can't back out now. You have to do this for Delaney whether you want to or not. I won't be the bad guy for you."

"I don't know if I can teach her, Ford. I'm sure you saw what happened to me. The whole world has. My hearing… it's not great right now. I didn't want to say no and upset her, but I'm afraid I will let her down."

"I did hear about what happened to you. I'm sorry." He wanted to tell her she would be okay, that she was resilient. He stayed away from words that would resemble too much caring and understanding. He had agreed to the lessons for his daughter. He had no intentions of even trying again for friendship with Nyx.

She stepped back. "Thanks. With my hearing compromised, I'm not sure if I'll hear the pitch."

"Well, I guess you'll have to figure something out. I can't believe I agreed to this, but I won't let Delaney down. She's been through enough already. The show is in four weeks. Just make her a little better than she is."

"Why aren't you helping her? You can sing."

"Because I don't have the time. Some of us have real jobs."

"Excuse me, I have a real job." She scooped her hair away from her face and held his gaze with hers.

"From what I heard, you had a real job. Now you don't have any job except to teach my kid how to sing. I don't like putting you two together, but it means a lot to her. Be at my mother's tomorrow at three. Don't make me regret this."

"I'll be there. And like I said, I'm not looking to get paid. Helping Delaney isn't a job. I'm cultivating a little girl's dream so she can believe in herself and take on the world whether it's to sing or make those adorable bows. You remember feeling that way? Like you could take on the world. Don't you?" She turned and headed up the street without looking back.

He watched until she was out of sight. Yeah, he regretted agreeing to this already. Nyx didn't know what she was talking about. When they had planned to go to Nashville together, they were teenagers. He had no idea what he wanted in life back then. Except that he had wanted her and wanted her to stay with him. Playing on stage in front of thousands of people was a child's fantasy that had not served him.

Whether he liked it or not, he would be in Nyx's company through Christmas. Or maybe Nyx wouldn't stick around that long. She didn't have the staying power. That could work out in his favor but would break Delaney. He didn't like the cards being dealt. Someone would end up hurt. He certainly didn't want it to be his daughter.

But he didn't want a repeat performance either.

CHAPTER FIVE

Nyx forced her legs to carry her up the street and away from Ford. Crisp air brushed against her like a taunting child on a school playground. Trees lined the street with their bare branches, unhindered in their nudity. The trees didn't know they were less than without leaves. Why couldn't she realize she wasn't less than without complete hearing? Because all she wanted now was her career back the way it was before. Her hearing problems meant no career existed.

The Victorian houses that lined the streets all decorated in their Christmas splendor did nothing to calm the chaos in her mind. Candlewood Falls used to host a Victorian home Christmas tour every year. She wondered if it still did.

She had tangled herself up in a real mess by agreeing to teach Ford's daughter to sing. She could barely sing herself these days and only when alone. Once music mixed in, she struggled to hear the key and stay in it.

She had to find a way out of teaching this child. That

was the only option. She didn't want to hurt Delaney's feelings, but there was no way she could help the little girl. A good enough excuse must exist somewhere if she looked hard enough to find it. She would have to think of something.

Nyx shoved her hands in her pockets and hunkered down in her coat. Besides the obvious fact that her hearing was a problem, this was Ford's daughter. She couldn't believe that Ford had a daughter and at the same time all he had ever talked about was having a family of his own. He had wanted a slew of kids. Did he have more? Was there a wife? Why hadn't she asked her mother these questions before Ruby's memory failed her? Nyx never allowed any talk of Ford to take up the time she spent with her mother. Big mistake. Big.

Seeing Ford on a regular basis would pop up memories like pimples before a photo shoot. Memories she had put away a long time ago. The past belonged to another girl.

She stopped short. Somehow, she was in the middle of the street. A horn honked. Tires screeched from somewhere in the distance but didn't register the way they should have. A truck with its dusty chrome grill broke inches from her. Too absorbed in thoughts of the past, she hadn't realized she left the sidewalk.

"Nicole, why aren't you looking where you're going, girl?" Her father leaned out the window of his beat-up old Chevy with so many miles on it the odometer had turned over. He was a paunchy man with little hair and what was left was white. His cheeks were ruddy, and his blue eyes watered.

She stood in the center of the road with no illusions

that he was upset because he almost ran her over. More likely the cold wind teared him up. She hurried to the sidewalk and sucked in a few breaths, slowing her rapid heart. She needed to pay better attention. She might not be so lucky the next time.

"Hi, Dad. Sorry about that. My mind was elsewhere." The motor sound in her ear matched the speed of her wild thoughts. She had been so fired up about Ford she'd put herself at risk. Every time she stressed out, the tinnitus worsened. It didn't take a genius to figure out she needed to calm the hell down.

Her father pulled over to the curb and rolled the passenger window down. "Where are you going?"

"I'm taking a walk."

"From the house?" His bushy white eyebrows jumped the creases of his forehead.

"No, that would be... never mind. Where are you headed?" She wanted to say walking from the house to the middle of town would be nuts, but what was the point? They didn't need to discuss her whereabouts.

"Stopping at Uncle Silas' place. Told him I'd bring by my miter saw."

"Can I come? I wanted to see the mansion." She should go back to her room and lock the door, keeping the world at bay. Better to research some way to tackle her problems. Talk of spending time with family was nonsense right now. The day had worn her out, especially seeing Ford without any warning.

"You want to ride with me?"

She pulled open the door and hopped in the seat. The door blissfully shut out all the noise of cars driving up and down. The ringing in her ears continued, but she might not have to focus so hard on what her father said. She could use a minute or two of not being on the street. That close call shook her.

"Yes, I'd like to ride to Uncle Silas', if that's okay with you?" She gripped the door handle. Maybe he didn't want her in the truck with him. She hadn't given that a thought.

He squeezed her shoulder and shook his head. "No. No. It's fine. You come along with me. Getting dark soon. You shouldn't be walking the streets by yourself."

"It's Candlewood Falls. I don't think I have to worry here." This was a safe town where nothing bad happened. Besides the fire at her uncle's and a problem her cousin Brooklyn had at the alpaca farm a couple of years back where she was threatened, the only other big thing to happen in town was her Uncle SJ's murder. She paused on that thought. Her family might be cursed or some weird thing.

"Well, with your condition and all. Not safe for someone like you." Her father faced her and held her gaze.

"What do you mean, *someone like me*?" She should quit while she was ahead. Picking a fight with him would do neither of them any good. He probably didn't mean anything by what he said, but the words rubbed her the wrong way just the same.

"I don't mean nothing at all. Don't read into it. You're just like your sisters, always misunderstanding me." He looked away, then pulled back onto the road.

She looked out the window without responding. Huck was the one who never seemed to understand, but she was tired of trying to explain and tired of being hurt by it.

The mansion was about a block up. They wouldn't have to be in each other's company for much longer. Uncle Silas would be the buffer for them. Nyx could take a look around since her curiosity seemed to have the best of her. She had no real reason to stop by other than she had to get out of Petra's place before she suffocated, and then she bumped into Ford which made her want to walk to Canada. He had a way of getting under her skin. After a quick tour of the new hotel, burnt as it was, she would text Petra or Ember to give her a ride back. Maybe they could help her come up with a good excuse to give Ford and she would be out of the predicament she put herself in with these singing lessons.

Huck pulled into the driveway. Her uncle and his girlfriend had restored the old mansion and turned it into a boutique hotel. The town needed something like that, quaint and full of charm.

Her cousin, Van, lived next door. She hoped he wasn't home and looking out the window. She only wanted to see her Uncle Silas, if he was even here. Too many Wildes lived in this town. Coming from a big family had its downside. Privacy was hard to come by.

She slid out of the truck and came around the front while her father grabbed something from the truck bed.

The front lawn had large tire tracks through it and the smell of burnt wood hung in the air. Her father had mentioned the fire had started in the kitchen which was in the back. The damage from the fire couldn't be seen from the front. The front of the building looked like an old-style mansion with its red brick façade and wood door with etched glass. All the shutters were a bright white, giving the sun a good surface to bounce off of and welcome in the guests that may never come now. This place would've made a nice location for the Christmas Showcase. Too bad about the fire.

"Pretty thing. Isn't it?" Huck stood beside her.

"It really is. I'm glad no one was hurt. What happens next?"

Huck shrugged. "Silas will fix it. Damage stayed in the kitchen which was lucky. But it will take a few months to get up and running again. Have to get the insurance company in here and then the estimates. Big process. Might not be open till spring now."

"This would've been a special place for the Christmas Showcase."

"Sure would have. Now we have to listen to Weezer crow with delight it's back at the winery. Far be it for me to say, but I'm sick of the winery. Let's go inside."

She went to the front door and tried it. The door swung open into a large foyer with a grand split stair-case. The burnt smell was worse here. She pulled her scarf up over her nose. Yellow caution tape crisscrossed over the entrance into the kitchen.

"Hello?" Her voice echoed back. She craned her neck to see into the other rooms. "Is anyone here?"

Huck ducked under the yellow tape. If he responded to her, she didn't hear it and didn't have the energy to ask him to repeat it. Either someone was here or they weren't. And if Uncle Silas was not on the property, then she would move on and catch up with him another time.

Her father reappeared in the kitchen door sans the

saw he brought into the house. "Silas is at the orchard. I didn't think you heard me."

"I did not. Well, if he isn't here, then I'll be heading out. Thanks for the ride."

"Where are you headed?"

"Not sure really." She had nowhere to go and no one to see. In a matter of minutes, her world filled with concert dates and album rehearsals and holiday parties disappeared like an icicle in the sun. People she thought were real friends had stopped answering her texts, except for Luther. Suddenly, her Christmas shopping became a lot easier. She hated it. So, why hadn't she responded to Luther? What was she really avoiding?

"I can give you a ride."

"Are you glad this happened to me?"

Huck narrowed his eyes. "What?"

"Don't pretend you don't know what I'm talking about. What brought me back home. Are you glad my career is over?" Her father had never been supportive of her decision to leave town at eighteen and follow her heart. He had wanted her to stay put, go to college, major in something he chose. When she had made it, he didn't come to one show even when she had sent tickets and secured a flight for her parents. Sometimes her mother came with one of her sisters, but often her parents gave the tickets to her sisters and Petra and Ember showed up instead.

Huck swatted her words away. "Why are you bringing this up?"

"I don't know, Dad. Now seemed like a good time. We're both here. At home, you try and ignore me. Deafness isn't contagious."

"I know that. I don't ignore you. You lock yourself in your room and don't come out. I don't know what to do about that. You don't want to tell me anything. You talk more to your sisters."

"Well, maybe that's because they give a damn." She should hold back, not start a war, because that was where this conversation would end up. He would make excuses and never take responsibility.

"I'm not talking about this now. We shouldn't even be here. The place isn't safe. I'm going home. If you want a ride, then you'll come with me. Otherwise, don't stay here." He turned without another word, dismissing her.

She opened her mouth to fight back, but the words died on her lips. The tinnitus shifted gears, as if it were an engine climbing a steep mountain. The motor revved and pulsed in her head. She shoved the heels of her hands against her ears, but the noise did not stop. Tears burned her eyes. Why had she come home? And what was she going to do to get back to her old self?

If her old self even existed anymore.

CHAPTER SIX

Ford tossed his coat onto the back of the chair in his living room. The house was warm. He had probably left the heat up this morning before they left. Delaney's dolls were all over the living room rug. Her crayons were scattered over the coffee table along with a half-empty cup of who knew what inside it.

He should hang up the coat and be a good example for his daughter, making his point hit home when he told her to clean up her messes. He didn't have the energy to set another example. Being a parent gave a new definition to the word exhausted.

He couldn't have Nyx in Delaney's life. How had he agreed to that? Maybe because he hadn't expected to find Nyx on the sidewalk talking to his mother and daughter. Seeing her had thrown him into a tailspin. Memories rushed at him, knocking him off-balance. Heat swept through him. His body broke out in a sweat. He had wanted to give her hell for breaking his heart and wanted to hug her because it had been too long and deep down in places he didn't like to admit to, he missed her.

A man his age should not miss his old girlfriend so much. And yet, to the dismay of his logical mind, he did. That didn't change how things were and he had to protect Delaney.

But first he had to make dinner. He opened the refrigerator. They were in desperate need of a run to the grocery store. Other than milk, a couple of eggs, and some soggy lettuce, they didn't have much. Another fail in the dad category. Single parenthood had its challenges.

Pizza it would be. He scrolled through his contacts for Angelo's Pizzeria and placed an order.

Delaney skipped into the kitchen. She had swapped out her red and green bow for a purple one with white polka dots. He had lost count as to the number of bows Delaney made. He hoped she didn't ask him to wear one, but he would with pride. He couldn't very well tell her to march to her own drum if he wasn't willing to wave the pompoms in her direction.

"I'm hungry," she said.

"I ordered pizza. It will be here in a half hour." He loaded the dishes from the sink into the dishwasher. After dinner, he had to answer some emails he didn't have time to address during the school day. He wanted to spend quality time with Delaney, especially since his ex-wife was barely in the picture. Some nights were harder than others when the demands of his job tied his hands.

"What is a half hour?" Delaney scrunched up her nose.

"What are they teaching you in school?" He abandoned his chore, then twirled his daughter in the air.

She squealed with delight. "Daddy." Her laugh mended all that ailed him.

He placed her on the stool at the counter. "How many minutes in an hour?"

"A hundred? Can I have a snack?" She stared at him with her big brown eyes.

"You had a snack at Green Bean. You don't want to spoil your appetite. Is one hundred minutes your answer?"

"Yes. Is that right?"

"Sorry. It's not. Let me show you." He pulled up an image of an analog clock on his phone and spent a few minutes going over how to tell time the old-fashioned way. She screwed up her face and looked at him as if he had three heads, but he persevered.

The pizza delivery interrupted his lesson.

"Yay, we can eat now." Delaney clapped her hands with a lot of enthusiasm.

"We'll practice again later." Later might be tomorrow, this weekend, or next year, but his daughter would tell time.

After dinner he put in a movie and answered those emails while Delaney watched on the couch beside him, leaning her head against his shoulder. She grabbed a blanket and threw it over herself and his computer.

"Sweetie, I don't want to use the blanket right now. I'm working." He tucked the blanket around her.

"You always work." She looked up at him with her bottom lip sticking out.

Guilt stabbed him in the eye. "I'll be done soon."

"You're not watching the movie."

"I can hear it." He tried to return his attention to the email.

She fidgeted in her seat, knocking into him. "Sorry." Her lips turned down. The bottom one stuck out again.

"It's okay. Can you find a way to get comfortable?" He had lost his train of thought and needed to reread what he had written.

She swung her legs onto the couch, kicking the computer right out of his hands. It tumbled to the floor with a thud.

"Delaney, watch what you're doing." He jumped up, unable to control the frustration in his voice.

She scurried to the edge of the couch like a rat blinded by the light and pulled the blanket over her head. The role of father was impossible, and he screwed up more than he didn't these days.

He closed his eyes and took a deep breath. "I'm sorry that I yelled. I know you didn't mean to kick the computer."

"It was an accident," she said from under the blanket.

Guilt took the ice pick out of his eye and stabbed his throat. He sat down beside her and eased the blanket away. Her bow was askew, and her hair stuck up from the static.

His time with his daughter was limited. In a few years, she wouldn't even want to be around him. She would lock herself in her room and talk to him in single syllables. Almost all of the parents of his high school students complained about their children morphing from a middle schooler into someone they didn't recognize any longer. He wasn't looking forward to that. Without a partner to share the responsibilities with, sometimes he had to work when he could be bonding with his daughter. If he became the next superintendent, his workload would increase, but he would get a raise and really have the opportunity to make the needed changes in the district. He would make more of a difference than just as the principal in a small town. And he would finally have the challenges he sought to feel satisfied at work. He loved what he did, but lately, work had become a grind.

"I will be more careful with my words."

"I'll be more careful with my feet."

"Deal." He stuck out his hand. She gifted him a giggle that sparkled like glass.

"I'm very excited about my singing lessons. I'm going to tell everyone in school that Nyx Wilde is my new teacher. All the kids will think that's lit." Delaney fluffed the blanket around her legs.

"Lit?" He often heard the high schoolers use the latest vernacular, but coming from Delaney, the term sounded foreign and out of place.

"Come on, Dad. You know. It's what people your age think is cool." She adjusted the bow.

"My age?" He was too aware of his age. Not that he was old, but time had passed by in a nano-blink. It seemed like yesterday when Delaney was only two, and now she was in the fourth grade with a mind of her own.

"Old. You're old, Dad." Her smile burst wide on her adorable face.

"Got it. You know, Nyx is my age." He wished she wouldn't go to school and say a word about her singing lessons, but he assumed she would. If he told her not to mention them, it would be a certainty she would. He didn't want her to feel badly if Nyx disappointed her.

"She's different. She's a superstar."

As if that explained it all. He shifted to look at her. "Delaney, Nyx hasn't been feeling well. I don't want you to be too upset if she can't follow through." He wouldn't go into details about Nyx's problems. That was her business. Nyx might want privacy, and he would respect that.

Delaney sat straight up. "Is she canceling? She said she'd be there."

"She's still coming. But I wanted you to know that if she does cancel it's because she's not well and not because of you." He had Delaney's self-esteem to think about. He didn't want her internalizing Nyx's choices as a reflection of herself. He doubted Nyx understood the impact she would have on an impressionable young girl. She didn't have any children and had always put her needs above his. He paused. These lessons weren't about him and Nyx. He wasn't being fair. They had been kids.

"Does she need chicken soup? We could bring her chicken soup."

"She doesn't need anything." Nyx never did. He was surprised by her return to Candlewood Falls. Even with the debacle on stage, he had expected her to bounce back. She never asked for help. To see her home, had him wondering how bad the hearing was now.

"Please don't let her cancel. Tell her I don't care if she has a cold, okay? She doesn't have to do the singing. She can just tell me what to do if her nose is stuffed up. I know what I'm going to do." Delaney jumped off the couch.

"What's that?"

"I'm going to make her a bow. That will make her feel better." Delaney ran around the couch with her hands in the air.

"Delaney, a bow won't help with what she has."

"Of course, it will, Daddy. Bows make everything better." Delaney pounded up the stairs. Her bedroom door closed with a thud.

He wanted to tell her not to stay up late and not to bother. Nyx would never wear a bow anyway. But he went back to his emails. He could take another ten or fifteen minutes to plan his day for tomorrow, and then he'd tuck in Delaney.

His mind wandered to Nyx and what she might be doing tonight. Was she curled up on the couch at her father's place? How was her hearing? His mother had given him Nyx's number. He could send her a text to confirm tomorrow and then slip in a question to see how she was doing.

He closed his laptop and went into the kitchen. He grabbed a piece of leftover pizza and ate it standing at the sink. Or he could keep his distance from Nyx as much as possible. They didn't have to be friends. They certainly weren't going to be anything more.

If he had any luck, she would cancel those singing lessons. Then he wouldn't have to deal with her at all. But Delaney would be hurt. That he couldn't allow.

He grabbed his phone off the table and typed out a text.

This is Ford. Confirming tomorrow. His finger hovered over the screen as he debated on sending. He wasn't trying to be her friend again. Not like before. This was just a parent confirming his child's schedule. Parents did it a million times a day. He sent the message.

He stared at the screen for a minute, but she did not respond.

Her silence could be for many reasons. It didn't have to mean anything.

And yet… it did.

CHAPTER SEVEN

Nyx jumped off the couch. Her phone had vibrated under her hand and startled her awake. She had fallen asleep watching television in the family room. Her father went out for the evening, leaving her alone. Having the house to herself was a nice change and something she missed since her return to Candlewood Falls.

Back in Nashville, she lived alone. After road trips on tour buses with her band, she craved her empty house. She had insisted Miles keep his own place, and she keep hers. Permanent relationships hadn't been her thing. She didn't want to find herself without a place to go if and when a love affair ended.

At first he had protested, but the blustering was for show, like everything Miles did. Without much fanfare, he quickly agreed to living separately. The ease in which he gave up on the subject should have been a red flag that he wasn't in the relationship through thick and thin. She wasn't either, it appeared. She hadn't bothered to argue when he said it was over and she hadn't been entirely surprised he didn't want to stand by her side during her hearing crisis.

The text was from Luther.

Checking in.

All good here. Thanks. She didn't want to go into the details now or complain about not wanting to wear the hearing aids. They helped in some circumstances, but not in all. She couldn't play music with them, and all she wanted to do was play music on stage with her band. She didn't want to accept her situation or find work-arounds. She wanted to return to the way it was.

When are you coming back? Don't like working with other artists.

She stared at the phone. Luther could do sound for a thousand other people, but they had become friends over the years. She appreciated his skills and his friendship.

Soon. Trying to find a way back. Trying but not succeeding.

Good. See you soon. Call if you need me.

She wasn't sure when she would be calling. That was the problem amongst all the others. She put her phone in her lap.

The room was dark and warm, but for some reason being in the house alone set her on edge. If someone came in the back door, she couldn't be sure she'd hear them. She hopped up and checked the lock. She had tried to tell herself nothing bad happened in this town, but what if it did? How would she know if she had an intruder?

The door in the kitchen that faced the back of the house and the acres of treed property was closed but unlocked. Her heart beat faster, but she was safe. The cold metal of the lock resisted under her fingers. She forced it until it clicked into place. Her father would need to oil that or something.

She returned to the family room and tried to focus on the closed captions of a movie she'd seen so many times she could recite. Her phone vibrated again, and she flew off the couch as if bit by a spider.

Or by a text from Ford McKay.

She hated spiders. The jury was still out on how she felt about Ford.

Golda must have given him her number, which normally wouldn't be a big deal. She had agreed to give a singing lesson to his daughter. Any parent would confirm. But he wasn't any parent and seeing his name, knowing he had written the text, shocked her right out of her seat.

She rubbed her eyes with the heels of her hands and sank back onto the sofa. Something was different. For a second, she couldn't place the difference, but with joyous relief, the motor in her head had changed to a much quieter ringing. She nearly burst into tears. Maybe the motor was gone for good.

She turned the television's volume back up. The couple on the screen lay on their backs and talked about their future. A piano accompaniment emphasized the emotion. The voices were less muffled—the constant *in a tunnel* sound—than earlier. Maybe she was better.

Her phone buzzed again. Ford must be impatient for an answer, but when she read the screen, her heart sank. The new text wasn't from Ford. It was from Miles.

Where do you want me to send the stuff you left at my house? He hadn't asked how she was or if she was okay. He

65

hadn't said he missed her or was worried about her. He wanted to be rid of her because now she was a liability, a weight around his ankle.

Burn it.

She didn't care what he did with any of her clothes or toiletries. She hadn't left anything of value there. Deep down she realized they weren't going to last. She hadn't been able to admit it. Miles was a great manager. Breaking up with him would have meant firing him, and she didn't want to go looking for someone new. Seemed the universe took care of that problem for her.

She grabbed her phone and a blanket and went onto the porch. If she could hear a little better, she would be safe out there. The night air was crisp and dry. The smell of woodsmoke drifted toward her. A fire would be lovely on a night like this. And so would having someone to share it with. Someone who truly loved her for her and not what she could give them.

What was Ford doing right now? Was he curled up on the sofa watching television with the love of his life?

She should respond to his text. Now was her opportunity to cancel. Better not to start anything she could not finish. Even though at this very moment, her tinnitus was tolerable, teaching Ford's daughter to sing was a mistake. She and Ford needed to stay away from each other.

Her fingers stilled on the phone. She hadn't come up with a suitable excuse other than her hearing problem and Ford hadn't seemed concerned about that. Well, she was. She didn't want to embarrass herself or be unable to help Delaney.

Ford had only wanted to keep his daughter happy.

Nyx could out and out refuse. She didn't owe anyone anything. Delaney would learn disappointment at some point in life. Learning sooner than later would only serve her in her adult years. Nyx knew that lesson firsthand.

Her fingers tapped against the screen. The message said what she needed it to, then she hit send.

He responded immediately.

Thank you. Delaney is very excited.

"You're a sucker, Nyx Wilde," she said to the night sky. "When it comes to Ford, you still lead with your heart."

And would pay with it too.

Her phone vibrated with another text from Miles. *I can't burn your stuff. Stop overreacting. Send me your address.*

Was she overreacting? Maybe. But she believed she was entitled to a strong reaction considering what had happened. When she was scared out of her mind that night at the arena, what she had really wanted was Miles to have her back. He had thrown her to the wolves and she had believed it would be okay. Nothing was okay anymore.

Every time she tried to search on the internet for ways to deal with her problem, a hot sensation circled her throat and sucked the air from her mouth. She had to limit the searching. The number of articles with suggestions, techniques, and options constantly over-whelmed her, but if she stopped searching, she would never find the answer she longed to have. She would come up with a plan. She had to.

The irony that Miles didn't know where she was didn't escape her. The man she had pledged to love for her life didn't know anything about her, couldn't guess where she would run to lick her wounds. Time to end this once and for all.

I don't want any of those things. Throw them out, she typed back. *And don't text me again.*

She waited for a response. None came and she pretended it didn't bother her. Miles' disinterest shouldn't matter. She was Nyx Wilde. Any man would be glad to be with her. Well, maybe once, when she was whole. Did she dare to believe the tinnitus might be better? The doctors could be wrong. They were wrong all the time. Maybe the entire episode from the stage till now had been temporary. She could be on her way back sooner than expected. She almost sent a text to Luther, telling him so, but she had some details to figure out first.

All she needed was a new manager. Her band would jump at another chance to be on the road. She had a few songs in her vault she could pull out to record. The industry would have questions, and she could make fun of herself. Most people had a short memory. Her fans would forgive her for running without so much as a goodbye.

Her mind worked overtime. Thoughts of Miles and the possibilities of returning to her career swarmed inside her mind. She couldn't sit still any longer. She itched to make something happen.

The motor noise in her ear may have changed gears. She paused but couldn't be sure if she had imagined the increase. She had too many ideas racing around like hornets. Candlewood Falls could be in the rearview mirror.

Back in the house, she rummaged around the kitchen for the car keys. Huck had removed most of Ruby's belongings, but for some reason he had kept her old sedan, and Nyx was grateful for the freedom the vehicle offered.

She would go for a ride and quiet her mind. The old car shimmied under her touch, but handled the road just fine. The streets never changed. The soft sway of the car lulled her. She navigated her way through town without effort, all the turns coming back to her like the lyrics of a favorite song. At this hour, most residents were snuggled up at home. She didn't have to share the road with anyone else.

Stopping for a quick drink wouldn't hurt anything. Taking a few more turns, she found Murphy's tavern exactly where it had been for decades. Not everything about a small town was bad. Christmas lights outlined the front door and the edge of the roof. Just a few cars sprinkled the lot. She parked in the back, away from the other cars, and hopped out. She pulled her knit hat down and turned up the collar of her coat. No one would notice her or expect her to come to the tavern.

The lighting inside the bar was dim. The paneled walls absorbed whatever glow flickered from overhead. Even the Christmas lights around the mirror behind the long wooden bar did little to add a gleam. A bready scent hovered like a fog against the low ceiling. The place was packed with people, and that surprised Nyx based on the number of cars in the lot. Had everyone walked?

She scanned the seating area, but didn't see anyone she recognized. A lucky break. Between her large family and the enormous River family, who owned the winery, she was bound to know someone. She hadn't even given the River family a thought until now. Seven children were in that clan, and she had grown up with a few of them, but they hadn't kept in touch except for the occasional comment on social media. Any one of them could be here and she would have to force her way through a conversation.

Several young people played pool in the back. *Young people*—every year someone in their twenties became younger and younger to her. A drum kit and amps were set up in the area where bands played. The volume in Murphy's was a low rumble, nothing that had her head splitting or forcing her to run for the hills.

She slid onto a stool at the bar by the door in case she needed a quick exit. The bartender bounced over with a huge smile on her face. Her ponytail swooshed with each step. The name tag attached to her Murphy's t-shirt read Flora.

"Hi, what can I get you?"

Nyx had to struggle to hear what Flora said. "A bourbon neat, please."

Flora replied as she turned away, and Nyx couldn't catch it all. The tinnitus was ramping up. She wiped her hands on her thighs and took a few deep breaths. Nothing bad was going to happen. She had to keep telling herself that.

A few guys in slouchy tees, hair that hung in their eyes, and dirty-looking jeans settled in around the instruments up at the front. The blond one slung a guitar over his shoulder and tuned up. The noise shot through her head like a hot spear. She ducked as if she could avoid the impact and almost fell off the stool.

Flora returned with the bourbon and a smile. Nyx could only nod her thanks and downed the shot. The liquid burned the back of her throat, but she gritted her teeth until the burning eased. The motorcade in her head continued.

The band fired up a classic rock tune that blew off the ceiling. The singer, not the blond, careened into the mic like an out-of-control car hitting a cement wall. The audience erupted into screams and applause.

Nyx jumped off the stool. Sounds crashed inside her head, and she needed the noise to stop. Throwing a few bills on the bar—hopefully enough—she shoved through the door and into the cold air. The silence was almost as painful. Her ears complained with a revving engine and a piercing nonstop ringing. The parking lot spun, and the bourbon demanded a return to the outside world. She dumped her head between her knees and gulped in air. She needed a minute. Everything would be fine in a minute.

"Nyx, are you okay?"

She squeezed her eyes shut. This was not happening. She hadn't recognized a soul in the bar. Murphy's was supposed to be a safe place for an hour or two. She took her time standing to make sure the bourbon wouldn't play any tricks on her and embarrass her worse. She brushed her hair out of her face to get a good look at the man before her, but it turned out she didn't need a clear view. She could picture him on command and without effort.

"I'm fine, Ford. Completely fine."

Her words a complete lie.

CHAPTER EIGHT

F ord didn't know what he was doing. He had run after Nyx without thinking. When she had come into Murphy's, he almost ducked out the back. No one knew where he went on Thursday nights and that's how he wanted to keep it. Thursday nights were his secret and the way he stayed sane in an uneventful world. How he had kept his weekly outing a secret in a small town was beyond him, but the patrons on open-mic night weren't exactly the parents of his students.

Now, Nyx stared up at him with those beautiful blue eyes. Her pallid skin sunk in around her cheekbones and the color had left her lips, but she could still steal his breath. Another mystery to him. And not because she was looking frightened and worried, but he didn't understand how after so many years apart, she could still turn his insides out.

He faced her straight on. "Are you sure you're okay? You look a little green around the gills." He tried to lighten the mood, but the glare she shot him said he had failed.

"I'm not drunk if that's what you're getting at." She took off her coat and flipped it over her arm.

The temperatures skated below forty and the dampness in the air gave every hard surface a gleam, but Nyx had sweat on her upper lip. "I wasn't implying anything. I… I saw you run from the bar. I thought maybe the noise was too loud for you. I'm sorry. I shouldn't have bothered you. Forget I came out here." He turned to go. What was he doing? This woman had made herself clear more than once in their lives that she did not want or need anything from him. He still hadn't learned that lesson.

"Ford, wait."

He turned back. "Okay."

"I'm sorry I bit your head off. I didn't think anyone saw. Least of all you." She waved a pointed finger at him.

He wasn't sure how to take that last part. He shouldn't take it any way at all, but he didn't like her tone, implying he was the worst possible person to bump into. "It's okay. I caught you off guard."

"I'll say." She rubbed her ear. "God, that damn noise is so annoying."

"What noise?" He did a quick turn, then realized he couldn't hear it.

"What? Oh. Never mind. It's not important. I'm fine. Really. Thank you for checking on me."

"Sure thing. I saw you inside… well, you know what happened. Can I get you anything? Or do you need a ride?" He wouldn't leave her in the parking lot if she

73

required some help. He could get her to wherever she needed to be or call someone for her, like her fiancé. Ford did wonder if that man he had seen in pictures with Nyx was in town.

"Why are you being so nice to me?"

"Honestly, I have no idea." He couldn't believe he said that. "Sorry. Poor choice of words. You looked like you were in pain or trouble. I couldn't just leave you."

"Always the good guy. Being a principal suits you." Her smile tilted, then dropped off her lips.

That comment stung. He wasn't going to address his being the principal. She didn't understand his life choices. "It's a good job. If you're all right, I should let you go."

He had to get back home too and relieve the sitter. He had stayed one set too many, but he hadn't been in a rush to return to his mundane existence of making lunch, laundry, and paying bills. Fatherhood was never his problem. He had wanted a ton of kids. The rest… the day-to-day grind without help from a partner, was nothing like the life Nyx lived—until recently, that is.

"Yeah, I should go. It's been a long day. Thanks again. I'll see you tomorrow?" She arched a brow.

He hadn't planned on showing up at his mother's during the lesson. He had the perfect excuse—work. Golda picked up Delaney most afternoons after school, and he stayed in his office until four or five before heading to his parents' house. He never had to see Nyx while the lessons went on, if he didn't want to. He wouldn't think about how much he wanted to either. Thoughts like that were a dangerous gateway to more thoughts.

"I have to work late. The girls' basketball team has a game. I like to make an appearance at all the home games."

"Oh."

He wasn't sure, but something that resembled disappointment crossed her face—or disgust. She could be disgusted with him. He had no way of knowing.

"Where did you park? I could walk you to your car. Wait. Did you drive?" He needed to stop being the pathetic nerdy kid he was in high school, desperate for Nicole Wilde to notice him. And when she had... his whole life had been made. She was funny and smart and fearless. All the things he didn't see in himself back then.

"Just because I don't hear well doesn't mean I can't drive. In fact, it makes me a better driver." She tilted up her chin.

"I didn't mean you couldn't drive because of your hearing. I would never think that. I wondered if you drove because one, I don't know if you have a car here and two, I don't know if a big-time singer still drives herself around. You might have people for that."

She dropped her chin and laughed. Okay, maybe not disgusted with him.

"I still drive myself whenever I can. I would drive the tour bus if they'd let me."

"Of course, you would. Same Nicole."

Her eyebrows shot up.

"Sorry. Nyx. Same Nyx."

"You can call me Nicole. I don't mind."

Yeah, well, he did. "Let's stick with Nyx. Good night." His brain tapped him on the shoulder and said time to go, buddy, before he made a real fool of himself and tried to hug her or pass her a note.

"Good night." She turned for the far corner of the lot.

He waited away from the glow of the parking lot light so she wouldn't notice as he watched until she slipped inside an older sedan and the car started. He could tell himself he would do that for anyone, man or woman.

The truth was he was worried about her. When the band had kicked up, she had curled into herself as if a bomb had gone off. She jumped from the bar stool and stumbled out the door. She may have yelled or something because the people near her had turned in her direction. He was pretty sure someone had their phone out.

Pain had hardened her face as she ran for the safety of a quieter place. Whatever had happened to her while on stage a few months back had to have been terrible. He wanted to help her, protect her.

Stupid really because Nyx wanted none of those things. Especially not coming from him. She could have any man she wanted. She would not want some middle-aged high school principal with a child.

Even if he had loved her once.

He went to his car and drove home, pushing aside any more thoughts of Nyx. He paid the babysitter, locked the house up, and climbed the stairs to bed.

Going out on a school night was starting to take its toll on him. He had to be up early and ready to deal with his teachers and the slew of other fires waiting for him on a daily basis.

He peeled off his jeans and tossed them on the chair.

Delaney had asked repeatedly for a Christmas tree.

He would have to find the time to do that and dig the ornaments out of the attic. What he really wanted to do was sleep all weekend.

He tugged on a pair of sweats and an old tee, then slipped under the covers. Alone.

This would be the fourth Christmas he and Delaney spent alone. His ex-wife had moved to Florida with her new husband four years ago. She usually took Delaney for two weeks in the summer, but the rest of the year it was just the two of them. Delaney had stopped asking when she could visit with her mother because her mother always had an excuse for her absence. Not long after Delaney had resigned herself to her new circumstances, the bows started. Six months ago, she began begging for singing lessons.

He tossed and turned, trying to find a comfortable spot, but nothing seemed to work.

The newfound interest in singing lessons had been his fault. He had always shared music with Delaney by playing his albums and playlists for her. That was how Delaney knew about Nyx. He hadn't meant to reveal how deep his own love went, though. They were having so much fun that day he had broken out into song, forgetting where he was. She had been mesmerized.

He could sing and play guitar. He wrote songs at one time. He snuck out on Thursday nights to see local bands play because he missed the scene. And Nyx still had the power to turn his tongue to jelly.

He fluffed the pillow and shoved it under his head. He was afraid encouraging Delaney in the music world would lead to a lot of disappointment, if she decided she wanted a career in music. He wanted to spare her that heartache. He was also afraid she would defy him and take off the minute she could.

He lay on his back and stared at the ceiling.

Losing Nyx that way was bad.

Losing Delaney like that would destroy him.

CHAPTER NINE

Nyx changed three times. "This is ridiculous. It's just singing lessons. And I'm not even going to be a good teacher." She tossed the sweater on the floor and rummaged through her suitcase for another.

Her sister Ember sat on the end of the bed, folding the other discarded items that Nyx had rejected. "You're going to be great."

"I don't know if I can hear the pitch." She threw her hands in the air. "I won't know if the poor girl is in tune or not."

Her phone buzzed in her jeans pocket. She dug it out, declined the call, and tossed it on the bed.

"Who was that?" Ember looked between the phone and her.

"No one."

"It's someone if that scowl on your face means anything. Was it Miles?" Ember retrieved the last sweater Nyx had tossed and folded that too.

"You don't have to clean up after me. You're as bad as Petra. And no, it wasn't Miles."

"I can't allow you to ruin these beautiful clothes. This must've cost you a fortune." Ember held up her red cashmere sweater she saved for special occasions and the holidays. It did, in fact, cost a small fortune, but she wasn't going to say so.

She would not celebrate Christmas this year other than a couple of small presents for her immediate family and only because they would torture her until she agreed to spend Christmas morning with them. Maybe she would sleep at Petra's house the night before. Nyx did not need to wake up and see old, crotchety Huck's face on Christmas.

"It's just a sweater. It doesn't mean anything." Her clothes didn't matter to her. She couldn't buy what mattered—a real relationship with a man, one who cared about her in the way that counted, or her hearing back.

Seeing Ford last night in the parking lot reminded her of the kind of young man he was when they were together. He cared for her, held her close, kept her safe. He loved her for her because she hadn't been Nyx yet. If anyone could call her Nicole, it was him, and that was why she had said as much. He had come out to check on her because he was a good man. Miles had never done that for her.

"Who was on the phone?" Ember asked, distracting her from her thoughts.

"I get calls from reporters and radio disc jockeys who want to talk to me about what happened. I don't want to talk to them." Her hearing problems weren't anyone's business, and if she could fix it so she could hear again to play on stage, what was there to talk about anyway?

"And Miles would've handled the reporters and questions, but thankfully you kicked him to the curb."

"Exactly. What do you think of this?" She had opted for an oversized black tunic with a scooped neck. She would throw on her low cowboy boots, maybe look casual but not like a total screwup.

She would need a new manager if only to have someone else handle the requests for interviews. She also had emails from venues about rescheduling dates and about a thousand fans sending her well wishes that should be addressed. All of that didn't include social media direct messages that went unanswered because she couldn't bring herself to respond. Running off that stage had complicated things. She should've pushed herself through that night and then quit. For now, she needed to get a hold of Mandy and have her assistant handle most of the communications. Nyx was not on her game. She needed to pull it together and fast.

Ember unwound her legs and stood before her. "Try this." She tied one side in a small knot, draping the fabric in front of her.

"Nice touch." The woman in the mirror who looked back at her wasn't too shabby considering what she'd been through. Unfortunately, her hearing was for shit.

"I brought over my gold drop earrings with the pressed flower inside. Do you want to borrow them?"

"This isn't a date. I'm a music teacher—not even. I was guilted into giving lessons to a little girl by her grandmother and that little girl's adorable dimpled smile.

I'm hoping this is a one and done." She would have to see to it that it was.

"You're only going to give one lesson?"

Nyx checked her phone. She was going to be late, so she hurried down the steps to grab the keys to her mom's car. Ember chased after her.

"Nyx, wait." Ember grabbed her shoulder and turned her around.

She hadn't heard the whole sentence, whatever that might've been, but she did catch the *wait*.

"I don't have time. Thanks for coming over and hanging. I'll text you later. Say hi to Raf for me."

"You can't only give one lesson. That's not fair. She's a kid."

Ember always rooted for the underdog, and normally Nyx would agree, but not this time. Delaney was Ford's daughter. Life was hard enough without having to see him for the next few weeks.

"Please don't lecture me. I'm nervous and the noise in my head is getting louder. I just want to get to Golda's house, give the lesson, and go. You can tell me what a Grinch I am later."

Ember stepped back and held her hands up. "I won't say another word. You're going to do what you want anyway. Just think about what your actions will do to Delaney whose mother up and left her four years ago and never comes around."

That new information sucker punched her. She didn't know about Ford's ex-wife except that there was one. What kind of mother didn't come around for her child? Their mother had been the constant, always waiting for them to come to her for what they needed.

Without her mother, she would not have been brave enough to leave Candlewood Falls all those years ago. Nyx had also watched Petra fight to the death for her daughter. A mother's love was supposed to be unbreakable. This woman who had abandoned her child had problems.

"Point made." She grabbed the keys and drove to the McKay's house on the edge of town where the families with lots of money lived.

The Chambers lived next door to the McKays. When Ember had told her that their cousin Brad was involved with Lyra Chambers, she had laughed out loud. Brad might run the orchard, might even be a good-looking guy if someone was into the tattooed, long-haired, big muscles type, but he was a farmer at his core, just like his daddy, with dirt on his boots and in his blood. Ember swore Lyra had changed and that Brad and Lyra were in love. Nyx would have to see it to believe it.

She pulled into the circular driveway and parked behind a white Lexus. The house rambled on each side of the large wood front door. Natural color stones accented the cream exterior. White pillars lined the cement front porch. An oversized Christmas wreath filled with imitation fruit and a gold bow hung on the door. White lights decorated the columns and draped over the precisely pruned bushes. This house always made her insides jitter.

As a young woman, coming here after school to study and to make out in the gigantic basement, her nerves would tie her up in impossible knots. She would drop things, spill drinks, choke on her food. Golda would always offer a kind smile without saying anything. But it was Ford's father who would wrinkle his nose as if she had passed gas at the dinner table.

Mr. McKay would ignore her and if she did get up the nerve to ask a question, his answers were direct without emotion or elaboration. He had made himself clear that she, Nicole Wilde, was not good enough for his son.

Well, she wondered what Grant McKay had to say after she had made the big time and everyone knew her name. Did he still think she was less than, not worthy of his only son? What Grant thought didn't matter. She had nothing to prove to him or anyone. Besides, Ford didn't want her in his life. Grant would not be an issue this time around.

She rang the bell.

Hurried steps charged toward the door. "Lolli, she's here," came from inside.

Delaney threw open the oversized door. Her smile could light up a ten-foot tree and touched each ear, igniting her dimples. A green bow with little red packages sat high on her curly-haired head. She wore a green sweatshirt and jeans. Her striped socked feet were also red and green. Nyx's heart melted. Only giving one lesson would be harder than she thought.

"Hi, Nyx." Delaney grabbed her hand and tugged. She had little choice but to follow the determined child through the door.

Golda clip-clopped in her high heels over the porcelain-tiled foyer. "Come in." She waved as she closed the space between them.

Golda was elegant as always in black slacks and a crisp white blouse. Her makeup was applied with perfection. Nyx second-guessed the five-dollar lip gloss she smeared over her lips before she ran out of the house.

"It's wonderful to see you, Nyx. May I take your coat?" Golda held out her hand.

"Thank you, Mrs. McKay." She shrugged out of her ancient wool coat. She didn't often need a heavy coat in Tennessee. When she came back to New Jersey, she had to pull all her winter things out of the back of her closet. The season was still officially fall, but December was cold and gray with the kind of dampness that seeped into your bones and took up residence until May.

"Nyx, dear, you really have to call me Golda. It's about time, don't you think?" Golda arched a perfectly plucked brow.

"Golda. Sorry. The house is still lovely."

The house was as magnificent as always with its large staircase. A living room waited to the left and a dining room to the right. The foyer reached back into a family room and kitchen area. She remembered the house well. Today a large Christmas tree was tucked into the corner by the staircase. Its top reached the second-floor landing. The tree exploded with ornaments.

"This is Lolli and Pop's tree." Delaney pointed to the oversized tree draped in gold and red ornaments, pretty enough for the cover of a magazine. "My tree is in the family room. But we're waiting to decorate it."

"This tree is beautiful. I'm sure yours will be too." She hadn't had a tree in forever. Living alone never inspired her to get one and many times she was on the road or she spent the holidays with friends who lived nearby her home in Tennessee.

"You can help us decorate it," Delaney said.

"That's very sweet, but I wouldn't want to intrude on family time. Are you ready to get started?" She still worried this was a huge mistake. The tinnitus was just a pulsing, swooshing sound at the moment. But she held Delaney's buoyant gaze and hoped this next hour would fly by.

"You two can practice in here." Golda stepped into the living room with its wide window that looked out onto the front yard.

Dusk was about to say good night to the pitch dark of evening. The antique sofa on the far wall was flanked by wood tables. Each held a porcelain lamp, ready with their lights on to push the darkness into the corners. The long room spotlighted a baby grand that gleamed.

"The piano has been tuned but doesn't get much play any longer. Feel free to use it. I'll be in the kitchen if you need anything." She turned to go but stopped. "Oh, before I forget." Golda pulled a check out of her pocket.

"No, thank you, Golda. I meant it when I said I didn't want to be paid. Let's see how today goes, okay?" She tried to lower her voice so Delaney wouldn't hear her. Nyx could barely hear herself.

Golda leaned in. "I know about your hearing problems. I don't care. Do your best. I want Delaney to be in that showcase on Christmas Eve. She needs the confidence boost. I love my son, but he's holding the reins too tightly. He needs to allow her to dream a little."

She didn't know what to say to that. Golda and

Grant had often told Ford to keep his dreams within reach. Lofty dreams would only bring about disappointment. They had been the reason he wouldn't come with her when she had left town. Something changed in this woman, and she liked it.

Golda held out the check. Nyx shook her head. She would not take this woman's money even if this was the best singing lesson in all the land. If her hearing was perfect, this lesson wouldn't be happening. She had never given a singing lesson before. *Why, oh why had she agreed to this?*

"Yell if you need me." Golda click-clacked away, leaving her and Delaney alone.

"Why do you call your grandmother Lolli?" She hesitated to get too close to the piano. She wasn't ready to touch any of the keys, allowing their deep vibration to penetrate her.

"Because of Pop," Delaney said as if this made all the sense in the world.

"Pop?"

"My grandfather. He's Pop. So she's Lolli. Get it?" Delaney's smile lit up her face.

"Lollipop. I get it. Cute. Did you come up with that?"

"I think my dad did. And Lolli. She said Pop needs to laugh more. He's a grumpy old man."

Clearly, nothing had changed for Grant McKay. Wonderful. "Is your Pop here?"

"No, he's at work. He comes home late." Delaney adjusted her bow that had slipped on her head.

"Do you have a favorite song?" She would let Delaney sing a few tunes, give her some directions, and head on out. Everyone would be happy, her most of all if she could be gone before Ford or his father showed up.

"I have lots of them."

"Great. Why don't we start with you singing one of those, and I can hear what you can do." She hoped.

Delaney tapped her finger on her chin. "Okay, I've got it. 'Nothing Compares to Us.'"

"Like my song?" The song she wrote about her and Ford, but never told a soul what the motivation behind the song actually was. She had been asked plenty of times, but always said the tune had come to her while being stuck in an elevator. The lyrics had come later, but it had been the other way around.

"It is your song. It's my favorite."

"Really? That's great. It's mine too. Okay, have at it." She grabbed a seat on the stiff sofa. This little girl was mature beyond her years and as adorable as a Christmas elf with those bows. Nyx needed to guard her heart or Delaney would steal it and Nyx would never be the same.

Delaney took a deep breath and broke out in song. The key was off. At least she could hear that much. Maybe because Delaney was just about shouting at her and causing her to flinch against the notes. Nyx held up her hand to get Delaney's attention. She felt a little like Simon Cowell during an *America's Got Talent* audition.

Delaney clamped her mouth shut. Her eyes grew wide, and her cheeks flushed a bright pink. Nyx's heart sunk. She did not want to do this.

"That was pretty good." She meant that.

"But you stopped me." Delaney fidgeted with the hem of her sweatshirt.

"I did. I love that you want to sing one of my songs. That's a big compliment. I'm not sure that's the right song for you, though. Do you have any other songs you like to sing?"

Delaney pressed her lips together in a thin line and shook her whole body no.

"You must sing other stuff. Who else is your favorite?"

"I don't know."

"Would you come sit next to me?" She patted the spot next to her. Delaney scooted onto the sofa. Nyx made sure to face her so she wouldn't miss anything Delaney said. The off-key singing had shaken the ringing in her ears loose. She might not catch all the words if she didn't focus.

"Your Lolli says you want to be in the Christmas Showcase. Is that true?"

"Yes." Delaney nodded hard enough to slide the bow off her head.

"Good. Do you want to sing a Christmas song maybe?" She could find an easy enough song for Delaney to master and it would fit the event well. There should be a pianist available who could accompany her.

"No. I want to sing one of your songs because I want to be a singer someday. Just like you are."

"That's a big dream. I wanted to be a singer at your age too. If you want to go for it, you'll have to learn about how music works. Do you know about the key and tempo a song is in?"

"Sure. I know." Delaney jumped off the couch and ran to the piano. Her hands pounded the keys before Nyx could stop her.

The loud noise vibrated through her head. She squeezed her eyes shut against the assault, but Delaney continued to pound on the keys, causing distortion in Nyx's ears. Delaney wasn't doing it on purpose, but Nyx had to stop her. She still wasn't ready to get back to her old life and that brought tears to her eyes.

"Delaney, stop that." Ford whisked into the living room and put his hand on Delaney's arm.

Silence spread through the room like a quiet snowfall. The ringing in her ears increased. Silence was often worse than the noise because her brain searched for the sounds she could no longer hear and tried to replace them, causing the unbearable sounds in her head.

"Daddy, I was showing Nyx about keys." Delaney stared at Ford as if he had three heads.

Ford's gaze bounced between her and Delaney. Words dried up on her tongue. He looked handsome in his suit and long wool coat. He had brought the smell of cold, wintry air with him. His tie was loose around his neck and the top button of his wrinkled shirt was undone, revealing the soft spot of skin between his collarbones. Half-moons the shade of eggplants hung under his eyes, and his jaw was dotted with a day's growth of beard, but he could still stop her heart.

"Sweetie, that was a lot of banging. Why didn't you play the song you do know?" He pulled off his coat and tossed it on a nearby chair.

"I don't know." Delaney pushed out her bottom lip as if she might be considering his question.

He turned to her. "I'm sorry to interrupt. I could hear that from outside. I thought you might need a little help." He tipped his head in Delaney's direction.

"It's fine. We were just getting started."

"Oh. I thought the lesson would be over by now." He checked his watch. "Do I have the time wrong?"

She had no idea what time he thought the lesson was, but he obviously hadn't wanted to walk in at the beginning. She didn't want him here for the whole lesson either.

"Golda was expecting me. I'm pretty sure I was on time."

"Meaning what?"

"Meaning nothing."

"No, you meant something by that comment. You think I can't keep my schedule organized or what... that I'm a helicopter parent? Are you worried I'm here to offer my two cents? I'm not, but I could, you know."

She had no idea what was happening here. "Hang on. I wasn't implying or assuming anything other than I was on time. It doesn't matter if you have the time wrong. You're here now and you can watch if you'd like." She wanted him as far away from her at the moment as possible, but if he insisted on sitting in, there was nothing she could do to stop him. Her head hurt. She was quickly losing all the energy she had mustered from focusing on his lips and ignoring the noise in her head.

"If you want to give your daughter singing lessons, then you should." She still didn't understand why he hadn't done that in the first place except that he didn't want Delaney to sing.

"Daddy, I want Nyx to teach me."

"Is everything okay in here?" Golda poked her head around the doorway.

"We're good, Mom. Thanks."

"Nyx, would you like a drink? I could make a cup of tea or a hot cider. Or something stronger, if you'd like." Golda gave her a reassuring smile.

"No, thank you. I'd like to finish the lesson if that's all right with everyone." And then she could get out of there.

Ford grabbed his coat and marched from the room without another word. Delaney's face fell. Nyx hoped Ford realized how his behavior affected his daughter. She knew firsthand what it was like to have to navigate a father's bad moods. When she was a kid and Huck was annoyed about something, everyone in the house had to tiptoe around him.

Golda stepped closer. "Delaney, please give Nyx and me a minute. Grab a cookie and a napkin and come right back." Golda kept her face pointed at her and didn't break their gaze.

A chill ran down Nyx's spine. Golda's constant effort to look her in the eye when she spoke unnerved her. What else was she tuned into? Had this woman seen inside her heart and learned that Nyx still loved her son?

"Okay, Lolli." Delaney skipped out of the room.

"I'm sorry about my son. He had a bad day at work. I hope you'll forgive him."

"You don't have to say anything. What's happening here isn't about him or me. It's about Delaney. I want to give her a couple of lessons before the showcase. She's going to need practice."

"Can you come back tomorrow?" Golda leaned against the piano and crossed her arms.

"Tomorrow?" She had repeated the word not because

she struggled to hear, but because she needed time to decide if she should return.

"Is that a problem?"

"I… I don't think so."

"My dear, if teaching Delaney to sing is too much for you with your hearing, then say so. I don't want you to do anything you can't. But if you can put up with Ford's mood for a few weeks, I would appreciate it."

She didn't want to sound like a complainer or a victim. Not to this woman. And she didn't want to give Ford the satisfaction of scaring her off. She would have to establish some parameters with him if this was to continue. The first one would be he had to stay out of the room while they were working. The second one would be his checking that temper around Delaney. She didn't deserve to get thrown in between their ragged past.

"I can help her. I'll come back tomorrow. Same time. Do you want us to finish today? We didn't get very far."

"Let's start again tomorrow, shall we?" Golda put a hand on her elbow and escorted her to the door. Somehow, her coat appeared, and Golda helped her into it. She opened the front door and the cold air whisked around them.

"If you're sure…" She wasn't. She wasn't sure what had just happened. But maybe this was better. They could begin again tomorrow without Ford there.

"Can I ask you a personal question?" Golda rubbed her arms. In that thin sweater, she must be cold.

"Okay." She braced herself for what was about to come next.

"Who is your otolaryngologist?"

She took a step back, not expecting that question. "Um… I don't have one in Candlewood Falls." She had seen several specialists in Nashville and in New York right after the incident on stage. The doctors had come well recommended with impressive credentials. The advice was hearing aids and learn to live with it. She didn't want to do the first and hadn't figured out how to do the second yet. She couldn't explain to Golda why she didn't want to wear the hearing aids. Maybe someday. But for now, they represented failure.

"Oh, dear, I doubt there is one in town. I was thinking Morristown or maybe New Brunswick where some of the best hospitals are. The top doctors work with those hospitals. Do me a favor. Please don't tell anyone I said that about our little spot of paradise. I love Candle-wood Falls, but one has to drive to find the right medical attention. If you understand me."

"I do. And I won't say anything." She agreed completely. She didn't know the town's new doctor, the one involved with Riesling River. Nyx was certain this new doctor was good, but if she needed something a little more specialized, she had to go to a city.

"Do you need a recommendation?"

"I'm fine. Thank you." She hadn't researched anyone in New Jersey yet. Until Petra had shown up and dragged her out of bed, she had stayed in her room under the covers.

"Don't be embarrassed. I can tell you're focusing on what I'm saying and when someone isn't directly in front of you, you shift. How bad is it?"

"Mrs. McKay, I'm fine. Thank you for your concern, but you don't need to worry. I'll be back tomorrow." She would not discuss the level of discomfort or lack of hearing with this woman and turned and hurried to the car.

The garage door closed in her peripheral vision. Mr. McKay must be home now. She really needed to get out of there and wished she had one of her vehicles with their updated features and not this ancient one. Her mother's old sedan still required she shove the key in the lock and turn.

Her hands shook and the keys fell, bouncing against the driveway. Did they make a sound when they fell? All she could hear was the ringing in her ears. Darkness had swooped in during the singing lesson and made finding the keys difficult.

She checked over her shoulder. She was alone. Golda must be insulted. She had even called her Mrs. McKay. Nyx squeezed the bridge of her nose and closed her eyes. She made a mess of all of this. Delaney deserved better from her singing teacher. Nyx just wanted to go home.

"Are you okay?" Ford stood inches from her.

She jumped and banged into the car. A pain shot up her hip. "Where did you come from?"

"The house. I called your name, but you didn't hear me."

What else was new? "Did you forget to tell me something?" She bolstered herself for the final blow of him telling her not to come back. She couldn't figure out why he had agreed to this arrangement and he was bound to end it, not only because their pasts were tangled in a knot that could never be pulled clear, but because she struggled to hear. Tears burned her eyes and she fought them down. She would not cry in front of this man for the things she lost, including him.

"I caught the end of your conversation with my mother and saw you run to the car. She can be a bit much at times. I wanted to make sure she didn't insult you or say something insensitive about your hearing loss."

She stared at him. Not once in all her time with Miles had he ever worried about the way someone else treated her due to her hearing issues. He didn't understand how humiliating it could be when she was in a loud room and she couldn't hear a conversation at the other end of the table. He would tell her to pay better attention to their lips or just talk to the person next to her, even if that person was a smarmy marketing exec from a competing record label. Until recently, she could make do with her problems, but when that motor began vibrating in her head, making do became nearly impossible.

Usually, what she would do in those uncomfortable scenarios was leave. Her abrupt departures from many social settings labeled her the elusive if not antisocial country singer. She didn't mind. The party scene had grown old in about five minutes.

"Nyx, did I lose you? It looked like you went off somewhere else." Ford narrowed his eyes. A crease deepened by his eyebrow. That was new. He was getting older, as was she, but in her mind's eye, he was or would always be that young boy who had stolen her heart with just one kiss.

"I'm here. Sorry. Your mother didn't do anything wrong. It's all good. Was there anything else?"

"Your keys." He bent down and grabbed the keys from behind the tire.

"Thanks." She fisted them and tried to smile but wasn't sure if her lips had behaved. She wanted to sleep for months. She unlocked the door and slipped inside.

Ford grabbed the door before she could close it. "There's one more thing."

"What's that?"

"I figured if we're going to be in each other's company for the next few weeks, for Delaney's sake I think we should try and get along. If you're up for it, we could go over to the winery and catch up. You can see the location for the showcase."

"I know what the winery looks like. I've been in the showcase."

"Right. Yes. I know. I thought it might be quieter there. We could go somewhere else. Your sister's place. Or Murphy's. Or we could take a ride to Clinton. Or not. It was just an idea."

Her heart reached out, wanting to touch him, but she pushed it firmly behind the cage of her ribs. He was still adorable when he became flustered, even as a grown man with beard stubble and chiseled features. She should say no. She couldn't handle being in his presence right now. It would be so easy to lean into him if he would let her. He was familiar and she craved the familiar—and a time when she was whole.

He waited for her answer. She should put him out of his misery.

"I'd like that."

His smile burst wide. "Great. How about Friday? I can text you a place."

"The winery is fine. Thank you for thinking of a quiet place."

"Sure. I'll see you Friday." He closed the door and stepped away from her car.

She followed the circular drive without looking back. By putting Ford out of his misery just now, she may have jumped right into hers.

CHAPTER TEN

F ord waited until Nyx's car was out of sight before going back into the house. He had not planned on asking her out. Temporary insanity took over him. He had sworn left and right after she broke his heart he would not so much as be her friend. Now, here he was grinning like the nerd he was because Nyx Wilde had agreed to go out with him. He shook his head and groaned.

"Real suave, McKay," he said to himself. He needed to remember this wasn't a date. He did mean it when he said they should get along for Delaney's sake. They could be friends this time, or acquaintances, but that was it.

"Ford, is that you?" his mother called from the kitchen.

"Yes. I'll be right in." The house he grew up in was still as sterile as a hotel lobby with its expensive, stiff furniture in the front rooms. The kitchen was modern with straight lines everywhere and nothing out of place.

He and his sisters were not allowed to make a mess when they were kids.

His mother plated chicken and vegetables, then placed it in front of Delaney who was on the phone, chattering away. His father came in from the other side of the room, holding his evening scotch.

"Hello, son."

"Hello, Dad." He and his father weren't particularly close. His father had always pushed him to go into his business, but that had never appealed to Ford. He didn't want to work with numbers all day even if those numbers equated to more numbers filling his bank account and living in a house like this.

"Who were you speaking with out in the driveway?" his father said.

"Nicole Wilde." He accepted the plate his mother handed him. He should decline the offer for dinner, but his stomach growled, giving him away. Eating here also saved him the task of cooking at home. He still had more work to do this evening. Work that he wasn't particularly interested in doing.

"Are we eating in the kitchen, Goldie?" His father looked around the room as if he had never seen the kitchen before and eating in it was preposterous.

"I don't see the point in dirtying the dining room for just us tonight. Have a seat, Grant." Mom pointed to the table with her serving fork.

His father ignored his mother and turned to him instead. "I hope you're not getting involved with that woman again. She's never been right for this family and now she's not well."

"Not well? Does she have a disease I don't know

about?" He couldn't help himself and had to egg on his father.

"Grant, please don't start." His mother rolled her eyes.

"She's not sick, Dad. She's suffering from hearing loss."

"She's deaf," Grant said.

"She's not deaf. She has hearing loss. She could go deaf someday, but that day isn't today." He never liked the way his father judged everyone who was different than they were. His father could not tolerate conditions that would interfere with what he thought a perfect child and family should be.

When Nyx and he were kids, his father always pushed for him to end it with Nyx and get involved with someone more like Lyra Chambers who grew up next door. Lyra was the homecoming queen, voted most popular, had come from money. Their families socialized together at the country club.

Nyx was a Wilde, and her father was Huck. The worst Wilde brother who owned that orchard. When her uncle SJ had been murdered, his father had said a tragedy of that magnitude bestowed a family such as the Wildes because SJ was a drunk who caroused with seedy people.

"Don't get involved with her. She won't help your chances for promotion."

"I highly doubt the board of education cares about Nyx. They want to know whether or not I have the district's best interests in mind. They'll be judging me based on my accomplishments." He could argue that Nyx would improve his chances. She could be a large benefactor to the school district, able to raise money or donate. He would not want a promotion based on someone else's reach.

"You're judged by the company you keep," Grant said.

The famous line he had heard his whole life. Even when he married Tenna, his father had passed that wisdom on, and when he and Tenna divorced, his father was happy to remind him.

"Dad, I'm too old for you to go around picking my friends." He fought the anger stirring in his belly. He wasn't hungry any longer and pushed the plate away.

"Just mark my words. She'll be no good for you. Stay away from her. She can't offer you anything in her condition."

"Dad, enough. I don't need your narrowmindedness right now." His voice carried across the room, and he regretted it the second Delaney stared at him with eyes as wide as a dinner plate.

"Daddy, Mommy wants to talk to you." Delaney held out his mother's cell phone. She adjusted her bow that didn't need adjusting. A habit she started when she was upset.

He forced a smile into his voice. "Thanks, honey." He took the phone and went into the living room.

"Hi, Tenna. What's up?"

"You haven't seriously brought your ex-girlfriend around our child, have you?" Her voice went through him like a shiv.

"What are you referring to exactly?" He suspected he knew exactly what she referred to, but he wanted her to say it. He wouldn't cave to her.

"Delaney just told me that Wilde woman was giving her singing lessons. You have to stop that immediately."

"Nyx is helping Delaney and no, I won't stop it." He may have wanted to earlier, but the second Tenna demanded he do it, he would never.

"After all we suffered, the reason we broke up, how can you flaunt her around our daughter?"

"Tenna, we didn't break up because of Nyx. Nyx was out of the picture long before I met you. We broke up because we want different things. You wanted your boss, and I wanted a committed wife who loved her daughter."

"I love Delaney. How dare you?"

He bit back the next words. Tenna loved the idea of Delaney. During her pregnancy, Tenna played the role of happy expectant mother to the hilt. But when she had a child to take care of, things changed. Delaney was no longer that shiny thing, but a real human who required diaper changes and middle of the night feedings.

He had begged Tenna to see someone in case her problem was postpartum. She refused. When the desire to be anywhere except with her daughter lasted years and he had discovered the affair, he told her to get out.

"Look, Delaney likes Nyx. These lessons will help her self-confidence." Which she needed, but he didn't say that to his ex-wife.

"Find another teacher. Even you. But not that woman."

"Why do you care? You didn't want me."

"I didn't have a chance in our marriage. I only wish I had seen it sooner. You have been in love with that woman your entire life. She was always the elephant in the room. I won't compete with her for my daughter's attention too."

"You don't have to compete for Delaney's attention. You're her mother. All you have to do is show up once in a while."

Tenna gasped.

"Look, I have to go. Nyx is staying. Deal with it." He ended the call and sank onto the hard sofa.

He couldn't figure out Tenna and what she truly wanted. She barely called to talk to Delaney. They saw each other once a year. He would not trade his time with his daughter for all the money in the world, and his ex-wife squandered hers. Deep down, he knew Tenna wasn't the motherly type. She was selfish and self-centered. The only reason she had loved being pregnant was all the attention bestowed on her. But he had hoped that she would prove him wrong. That once she saw their beautiful daughter she would change. She hadn't.

He looked up to find his mother in the room. He hadn't heard her enter. She handed him a rocks glass filled with a shot of bourbon. "Your voice carries," she said.

He downed a gulp. The liquor burned his throat but cleared his head. He didn't care what Tenna said. Nyx stayed—for Delaney. "Did Delaney hear me?"

"I don't think so. She's pattering on about Nyx to your father." Golda smoothed down her skirt.

"Great. He must love hearing all about Nyx after what he just said to me."

"He had the decency to let her go on and on without comment. Plus, I shot him a death glare when he tried to stop her."

"Why can't he do that for me?" His father had rarely shown a softer side of himself to any of his three children. His sisters dealt with him by staying away. He had left Candlewood Falls too, all too happy to put the small town behind him, but when Tenna left, he found juggling a full-time job and a small child almost more than he could handle. He came home so his mother could help him.

That had been one of the most humiliating days of his life.

She sat next to him and patted his knee. "Your father sees himself in you and wants you to accomplish more than he ever could."

"He has a funny way of showing it."

"He's far from perfect. I know this. And I've often thought about leaving him, but then I feel sorry for him because he would have no one if I left."

"You want to leave Dad?" Never in a million years would he have guessed his mother even entertained an idea about divorce. Divorce was for other less accomplished people, not for the McKays who were bred to be the best at everything.

"Some days. That's marriage, darling. And when you find the right person and you've spent forty years together, you'll have those days too. I don't agree with all of your father's sensibilities but he's a good man who has provided for his family and loves them. Even from afar. I've tried to soften him, but he's stubborn. I think the best chance we have at seeing some of that armor crack is your sweet Delaney. She's been asking him to wear one of her bows again. Not just the ties." Golda giggled, setting off the crow's feet around her brown eyes. His mother was still beautiful.

"I'd pay to see that." He finished the bourbon. "I should go. It's getting late. Thanks, Mom."

"You didn't eat." She stood beside him.

"I'll take it to go. I have work to do."

"Have some fun, Ford. You aren't getting any younger." She winked and brushed past him.

He did need some fun. Life had been hard. Good, but hard. He was ready to change that. Friday night could be the start. He wouldn't expect much. Nyx would never promise anything. She had stopped loving him a long time ago. They could be friends. Two friends out for a leisurely night. Nothing special had to come from it. Just a little pleasure.

To hell with what his father or his ex said.

CHAPTER ELEVEN

Nyx lost track of time. She hadn't meant to close the Bridgewater Mall. Well, stay through closing that was. She had wanted to do some Christmas shopping for her sisters, their men, and her niece Paige. She managed to find a sweater for Huck that he wouldn't cluck at. She hoped. She bought herself a pretty blue blouse that brightened her eyes. Her pale pallor and dark circles were evident no matter how much concealer she tried. Sleep still gave her issues because she paid too much attention to the tinnitus and found herself tossing and turning half the night wishing for quiet.

She tried white noise last night. That helped a little, but she was quickly realizing she couldn't go around with a white noise app playing all day. She didn't dare entertain the idea that the doctors were right and her hearing would never go back to the way it was. She had to find a way.

While she shopped, trying on clothes, smelling all the perfumes, and stopping in the makeup store for a new eyeshadow and lip gloss, the sounds in her head slipped into the background as if someone had opened a door and swept them outside. For a few hours, she relished the normalcy of her activities. She hadn't struggled to hear the cashiers. She even sang along with the piped-in Christmas music, but under her breath.

No one came up to her. Either the local people didn't notice her, which was perfect, or her fans didn't live in this area, or she was already forgotten. What would she do if her return was met with a tepid reaction? Could her fans be that fickle?

Her phone had been silent most of the day as well. Only Luther had texted to check in on her again. She should invite him to Candlewood Falls to meet her family. Too bad she didn't have an aunt to hook him up with. Luther was older, recently divorced, smart, an all-around great guy. He would like the small town and all its charm. Most everyone fell in love with Candlewood Falls, the town that whispered in ears like an old lover.

The day of shopping had been good, and she hadn't wanted it to end. But then a sales associate tapped her on the shoulder and told her the store was closing. Heat had stung her cheeks because she didn't know if there had been an announcement and she missed it, or she had simply lost track of time having fun for the first time in ages.

She had gathered herself and walked through the mostly empty mall to the exit as if her feet floated above the ground. Even with overstaying her welcome and being asked to leave the store, she kept her head high. Tomorrow night she had a date.

Not a date. Just two old friends getting together for a

glass of wine. She and Ford were a thing of the past. They had tried friendship once, and she had been happy to keep him in her life even if it was at a distance. He had struggled with being put in the friend zone and she couldn't promise him more back then. If he had followed her, then she would have jumped at the chance and jumped him, but he had stayed firmly planted in a secure life.

The security guard unlocked the glass doors to let her out into the parking lot. He was an older man with a paunch hanging over his belt and a limp to his walk. He smelled like peppermint and rubbing alcohol. But his smile was genuine and it reached his bloodshot eyes.

"Thank you." She slipped past him into the chilly night.

"Would you like an escort?"

"No, thank you. I'm fine." She hadn't parked that far away and there must be other shoppers still leaving with their Christmas packages in tow. Besides, she didn't think this man would pose much of a threat to a would-be mugger.

"Are you sure? I don't mind the walk. These old legs need a good stretch." He tapped his thigh. His smile grew wider. He was probably someone's grandpa who hadn't seen trouble in more years than he could count.

"Really, I'm good." She might have left Candlewood Falls to get to the closest mall, but she was still in a safe town. Of course, if she had her own car, she would have remote start instead of her mother's ancient thing. She would have to find a way to get one of her vehicles up here. She really needed to get her stuff together and decide what she was going to do. Stay in Jersey or go home. Though, Nashville didn't feel like home anymore. How quickly that had changed, or had it always been that way?

"Merry Christmas, then," he said, dragging her away from her thoughts about home.

"Merry Christmas." She switched her purchases to one hand and dug her keys out of her purse with the other.

The guard locked the doors and ambled away into the dimness of the mall. She watched until he was out of sight. The wind picked up and blew her hair across her face. Dried leaves circled the ground in front of her. Not a single car drove by. She was on the side of the mall without a restaurant. On this end, no one came or went.

The parking lot stretched out before her. Her car was the only one in this lot and all the way at the other end near the exit road. Had she really parked that far away? She must have, but the lot had been full when she pulled in earlier. She hadn't thought anything of her choice while the sun was still in the sky. Too bad she hadn't picked one under the light or away from the row of bushes blocking the road and her view to the street.

Her heart picked up speed. Would she be able to hear someone if they came up behind her?

That thought startled her. She wasn't sure why the frightening idea of a stranger appearing out of nowhere to cause harm invaded her headspace. Maybe it was the empty and scantily lit parking lot. Or the reality of her loneliness coupled with her vulnerability. She was a famous person who couldn't defend herself in the dark all alone.

If someone approached her, it wouldn't be the way

Ford had in his parents' driveway, with her needs as his first concern. No, it would be someone who meant to take from her what was not theirs to take.

No one was with her to help if she needed it. The guard was gone. She was alone in a parking lot where someone could hide behind a tree or in the bushes or under her car. Hadn't she read an article about a woman whose ankles were slashed because a killer waited under her car?

A shiver ran over her back. What if she dropped her keys again?

The wind continued to run through the bare branches, numbing her fingers. The Christmas lights wrapped around the trees did nothing to calm her and added no light whatsoever. A car turned off the exit road into the lot and stopped near her car. She couldn't move.

She was vulnerable against the things she could not hear and those that she could see. The motor in her ears revved, as if a truck struggled uphill. The earth spun and took her stomach with it. She closed her eyes to get her bearings and took a long breath. She could not get sick now. The car was gone. It's taillights winked in the distance.

"I can do this. It's just the mall. I'm safe." But her insides vibrated a different tune. She pulled out her phone but shoved it back in her coat pocket. This was stupid. Who was she going to call and wouldn't it be better to pay attention to her surroundings than talk to someone?

Her feet wouldn't move. She couldn't do it. Someone could be right behind her. She spun around to double-check that she was alone and caught her reflection in the glass. A short scream escaped her lips. She needed to pull herself together.

"On the count of three, you're going to run." Her voice came to her down a tunnel, but at least it was there. She wasn't completely alone if her words could come back to her.

She didn't bother to count and bolted. Her bags banged against her leg. Her purse bounced off her side. She kept her gaze on the car and the keys in her hand. She prayed she wouldn't drop them. Sweat ran down her back even in the cold.

She didn't dare turn around to find a figure coming up behind her. An angry fan who wanted their money back. That reporter who wouldn't stop dogging her. Or just a crazy person who abducted women alone late at night. She willed away the sensation of someone's fingertips scraping her neck. Her imagination ran away like a lunatic.

With trembling fingers, she fought to put the key in the lock and turned. She threw the packages in and dove onto the driver's seat. She closed the door and locked it. Her heart pounded in her throat, choking her. She rested her head on the cool steering wheel until her breath evened out.

Fear had come out of nowhere and took hold of her as if it were the stranger attempting to do her harm. It didn't matter that no one had followed her to the car and she was safe. She believed it was possible for a stranger to attack her because she could not hear them and take care of herself. If her hearing became worse, if she lost it for good, she didn't know what she would do.

If she couldn't get her hearing back, what would

happen? Her career would certainly be over. More importantly, she didn't want to be completely deaf, trapped in a dark silence. She needed help. And she needed it now.

❧

The earlier euphoria of shopping without the noise in her head was long gone. Nyx let herself into the house through the side door, locking it behind her. The kitchen was dark except for the light over the sink. The counters were wiped clean. One dish and cup dried in the dish basin. That lonely dish was what became of her father's existence without her mother. She missed Ruby and her soft voice and warm hugs. She would give anything to spill all her worries and have her mother help her clean them up.

Her father left something wrapped in aluminum foil on the table with a note.

Dinner. If you're hungry.

She was not hungry. All she wanted to do was climb into bed and sleep until the new year. Longer if possible. The blue light of the television flickered against the wall in the dark living room. Huck was asleep on the recliner. She tiptoed past the room and went upstairs.

In her bedroom, she locked that door too. Not because her father would barge in uninvited. He hadn't walked into her or her sisters' rooms since they were teenagers. He feared he would interrupt them changing. She locked the door because of the parking lot. Stupid. She dropped her bags on the floor and discarded her coat over the chair. She tugged off her boots and left them where they landed.

She had one more thing to do before she could pull the covers over her head and fished her phone out of her purse.

I'm sorry. I have to cancel our dinner tomorrow. Not feeling well. She hit send and the text to Ford could not be taken back. She hadn't lied. Her body ached as if she had a high fever. Her eyelids were heavy with fatigue. The motor in her head was accompanied by a high-pitched ringing.

I'm sorry you don't feel well. Is it the flu? The flu is going around at school. I could bring you chicken soup.

She almost laughed. He looked out for her, and she couldn't figure out why. They had basically been strangers all these years.

Not the flu. She debated on telling him everything that happened. He understood what her hearing problems did to her. He didn't pity her either. He hadn't said one thing to make her feel as if she were a burden or broken.

Stomach bug? Crackers then.

Hearing. Noise off the charts. She hit send and for the first time since the parking lot, a calm settled over her.

Can I help?

She wanted to say he could come over and climb into her bed like he did when they were teenagers. He would sneak in late at night when everyone was asleep. If her father had ever caught them, Ford might not have lived to see full adulthood, but they had never been caught. Except for the one time Ember bumped into Ford outside when she was sneaking in after her curfew.

No. Thanks. Tired. Going to bed.

Early?

Not for me. She went to bed earlier and earlier since she'd been back in Candlewood Falls.

Alone?

She dropped the phone as if it were hot. It bounced off the bed and landed on the floor. Her sweaty hands slipped over the case. She reread the screen twice to make sure she hadn't missed what he sent. What did he mean by that? One word could lead her into a thousand different directions. She wasn't sure she wanted to follow any of them.

Why would I text you if I were with someone? She should shut off the phone and forget this conversation. He could mistake what she said for flirting. Or worse, she had mistaken his question for the same.

Good point. Safe for me to come over?

He couldn't come here. How would she explain him to Huck who would wake at the sound of the door? Her gaze searched her messy room. He definitely couldn't see her room in such disarray. She should have let Ember and Petra clean it. What was she thinking? She could not have Ford over. They were barely friends, and it would stir up trouble. She had enough problems without inserting him into her mess.

You want to come over? Her fingers had a mind of their own, apparently.

Since you don't feel well. Better to have company. Unless your dad is there taking care of you.

This time she did laugh. Huck was not the hands-on kind of dad. When she or her sisters were sick, he was nowhere to be found. Her mom was the one who sat up all night, rubbing backs, administering meds, sleeping on the floor next to their beds.

Huck is asleep. Not exactly the nursemaid kind.

So? You want company?

Delaney?

Stayed at my parents.

She typed no but didn't send it. She stared at the screen as the cursor blinked, taunting her to take a stand. Ford in her house again would be a mistake. But she didn't want to be alone after the night she had.

Nyx? Still there?

She backspaced over *no. Yes.*

Is that yes, you're there or yes, come over?

Yes... to both.

CHAPTER TWELVE

He had lost his mind. Ford stared at his phone. What had possessed him to invite himself to Nyx's?

He hadn't wanted her to cancel. When he read her text, his heart sank. Meeting her for dinner was the highlight of his week after the argument with his father and Tenna. His teacher at school still would not handle the student situation the way he instructed, and he was being pushed into having to write her up. With the winter break only weeks away, the students were already itching for the term to end. No one wanted to sit still or study, especially not the seniors who thought June was already upon them. He had to break up two fights this week.

Way back in the old days, he had been confident of his feelings for Nyx and hers for him. It was only after she had left him, attempted to take him back, and then relegated him to friends only that he started to doubt himself. Once his marriage went bad, he wasn't sure if he had any idea how to handle a woman.

He hurried around the house, gathering his wallet and keys. He shoved his feet into his sneakers. He wasn't exactly dressed for a night out in sweats, but there wasn't time to change. She could easily text, saying she didn't want him after all. What he was rushing to, he wasn't sure. That didn't stop him from turning out a couple of lights and jumping in his car.

He could find his way to Nyx's house with his eyes closed—Nyx's old house. He didn't know if she would stay in town or go back to Tennessee after the holidays. His hopes needed to stay low. He hit the brakes. Was he hoping something would happen between them tonight? They weren't kids anymore, and he wasn't sneaking into his girlfriend's house. The present was not the past.

Maybe he should turn around. But she had said her tinnitus was acting up. She had to be frightened even if she didn't say. She wouldn't. Not Nyx. He wanted to be there for her. That was all he ever wanted. They could be friends. What was wrong with friends?

Everything.

Most of the houses on her street were decorated for Christmas. Many of them were set back from the road like so many roads in town. He could still make out lights around porches and roofs. Someone had decorated a ranch rail fence near the property's edge. The only dark house on the street was Huck's. That guy was as sour as they came. Huck would not be happy when he found out who was at the door.

He had to pull in the driveway. Parking in the street was too far from the house, but he stayed in the darkness, out of the way of the porch light. He sent another text to Nyx from the safety of his front seat. *I'm here.*

Be right down. Don't ring the bell. Huck sleeping.

He stepped out of the car and waited by the hood. The front door opened and she slipped out, closing it behind her. She hurried down to him.

"Hi." Her smile lit up her face and put a sparkle in her blue eyes. She wrapped a wool blanket around her shoulders. Her dark hair fell down her back.

He loved her long hair and was glad she had never cut it. He could still find a million reasons to like her. He had wanted to stay mad or at least indifferent, but neither of those things happened when he was around her. Enough time had passed to scar over the wounds that were nothing more than memories now.

She was as beautiful as the day he met her sophomore year of high school. He had transferred to the public high school from the private school he had attended his whole life. He wasn't sure how he ever convinced his parents to agree to that, but luckily, they had. Nicole Wilde walked into his band class and life changed forever. He had to pinch himself when she had agreed to go out with him back then. He might have to pinch himself now.

"Hey." Words failed him much as they did back then whenever he bumped into her in the hall. Tonight, he should have brought coffee or donuts or flowers—not flowers.

"Do you want to sit?" She pointed back to the porch with the swing that sat in the shadows.

"If you do." He would prefer to sit under the porch

light, where he wouldn't get any ideas about taking her hand.

She headed up the driveway and he followed. He should have followed her a long time ago when she had asked him to get on that train.

She took a seat and made space for him. The swing creaked under his weight. He put his arm on the back to steady himself but moved it and rested his hands in his lap instead. She smelled like berries and whipped cream and his mind formed images he had no business thinking about. He was definitely feeling like high school all over again.

"Thanks for coming over. I wanted the company more than I thought." She turned to face him.

"How are you feeling?" He couldn't stand the idea of not seeing her tomorrow. She would be at the singing lesson, and if he timed it right, he could be there before it ended, but that wasn't enough. She was in town, and he had to see her just a few times before the muse called her and she left him again.

"Surprisingly better now. You don't sound so far away which was why I didn't mind sitting in the dark. I don't feel like I have to focus on your lips. It's so weird, but my hearing comes and goes. Earlier today I felt normal."

"You are normal."

"You know what I mean." She dropped her gaze and tugged on the edge of the blanket.

He tilted her chin until she looked right at him. "I do. But do you?"

"What do you mean?"

"Hearing loss doesn't make you abnormal." He

wanted to go on touching her, but dropped his hand back to his lap.

"How do you know the right thing to say?"

"I say what I feel. You have a new struggle, but you are still you. Hearing loss doesn't have to define you."

"It's doing a good job of it these days. I halted my career, pretty much ending it. And tonight I scared myself so much I couldn't stop shaking until your text came through." She told him about what happened in the parking lot at the mall.

"My text helped?"

"Don't let it go to your head, but I always felt safe around you. You never let anyone make fun of me for being the kid who went around school, singing in the halls like a weirdo and the girl in the plays who carried Playbills instead of her books."

That compliment went straight to his head and a couple of other places too. "I admired you for being completely yourself. I never could do that." He still wasn't doing that completely. No one knew he went to open mic nights because he occasionally dreamed of a life not chosen.

"Do you like being a principal?"

"It has its ups and downs. The kids are great. Some of the teachers make my job harder. A few parents too." He wanted to unload all of the stress he had been carrying since his decision to apply for the superintendent job. Until now, he hadn't wanted to talk to anyone about it because it was easier to say things were fine even when they weren't. But he couldn't ask Nyx to deal with his stress when she had so much of her own going on.

"I bet you're good at it."

"I'm okay."

"So, what's it really like, having all those kids calling you Mr. McKay or hiding when they see you coming because they've got pot in their backpacks?"

"What do you mean? I just told you." Though those things did happen. The pot part more often than he liked.

"No, you told me the answer you rehearsed for the right audience. That crease between your brow gives you away. It's deeper now, by the way."

"Gee, thanks."

"I'm sorry. I don't mean it's bad. I like you older. You grew into your classic good looks with your slicked back hair, a little longer at the nape of your neck. That simple goatee you sport that someone has to look twice at to make sure they see it. You've got that swagger to your walk now. Almost like the cowboy has come to town. It's a good look on you."

"Well, thank you, but I think you've been in Nashville too long. I'm not a cowboy."

"You could sport the hat. I'll get you one. Tell me the truth about your job." She pressed her finger between his eyes as if she could rub that wrinkle away.

The jolt from her touch ran across his head and down his spine. All thoughts of work jumbled in his mind. He wouldn't be able to form a coherent sentence if his life depended on it. He had to use all his effort to keep from pulling her into his arms and kissing her.

"If you don't want to talk about it…" She looked away.

He turned her chin so they looked at each other again. He didn't want her to miss anything he said. Ever. "After a long day, I'd rather not rehash it. Being a principal is like any other job. It has its good side and its bad."

"Are you happy doing it? Can you imagine doing anything else?"

"Oh, Nicole. Let's not go there, okay. It's a good job that provides for my daughter."

"You called me Nicole."

"Sorry. Nyx."

"No, I like when you say it. My name sounds right when it's coming from you."

He had said her name a million times in his head. Maybe Tenna had been right about Nyx being the thing between them. He had never been able to shake her free even when those memories should no longer matter.

He stood and leaned against the porch railing. He needed some space because he really didn't know what he was doing here, sitting in the dark with her. Being with her was the one thing that could settle his nerves and calm his soul, but it also confused him now. They weren't who they used to be. He needed to stop trying to get there.

"Do you play anymore?" She wrapped the blanket closer.

"No time."

"But you loved it."

He loved her too once, but that didn't mean he could tell her or be with her or show her. When she left town and he went off to college, he put his guitar in the attic and allowed it to sit there for years. He had convinced himself he didn't miss it. That six-string was not his friend and only the lucky few had the chance to play in front of thousands. He didn't have that kind of luck or talent.

When Tenna left him and he returned to his home-town, he went into his parents' attic and retrieved the Gibson, dusting off the case with the care given to someone who had been lost and then found. He didn't play it though. If his fingers slid over the strings, he might not ever survive the choices he had made and had to live with.

"It was a child's dream."

"It was our dream."

"It was your dream. And you made it happen. You accomplished everything we talked about. That's enough for me." He had only wanted her to be happy, even when he had asked her to stay that humiliating night at the train station. But that person who had asked Nyx to give up what was in her heart had been a scared boy afraid to lose the one good thing in his life.

Nyx was too big for this town and for him. She lit up every room she walked into with her vibrancy as if the sun were clipped to her back. He realized that later when he had some time to grow up and become a man. Now, sitting with her, and seeing her at his mother's, that light had dimmed. She might know him, but he knew her too.

"You should play again," she said.

"Maybe someday. For now, I have Delaney to raise." He had no interest in dragging up old ideas that didn't fit any longer. Music wasn't a life for him. He was plenty happy watching from the seats—or he kept telling himself.

"Ford, do you ever wonder..." Her gaze traveled after her words.

"Wonder what?"

"What life would be like if we had stayed together." She came to him and stood inches away.

He had wondered that very thing while sitting in traffic and one of her songs came on the radio. He wondered what their children would've looked like and what it would be like to wake beside her every morning, watching her stretch and smile at him. He wondered if they would still laugh after all these years or if they would've broken in two anyway. He did not regret having his daughter—Delaney was his life—but in the quiet hours of the dark morning, when no one was awake anywhere except for him, he allowed his mind to wander into dangerous territory. If he had been brave enough to get on that train with her, life would have been very different.

"Nyx, the past is the past. We both made our choices." If he tilted his head down, their lips would meet. Would they taste the way he remembered?

"We were nothing but two kids who dated in high school for you? Is that what you're saying?" She stepped back and the cold air swooped between them, taking his curiosity about that kiss with it.

"You know that's not true. But we can't change what's already happened. Why focus on that?" Anger pushed his spine straight. She tortured him with that question. He had begged her to stay. When they tried again, this time long-distance while he was still in college, she had been the one to leave him, breaking his heart in so many pieces he had never found them all.

"I shouldn't have said anything about us. I'm sorry.

It's just with all that's happened lately, I thought maybe I made… Never mind."

"Maybe you made what—a mistake leaving me? Twice. Every time your life turned on its head, it's been me that you reached out to. Lucky for you it's only been twice. Or maybe lucky for me. What am I to you? Your consolation prize?" He did not want to be anyone's second choice, and he would always be hers. It had been a foolish idea to come here.

He brushed past her. She grabbed his arm. Tears filled her eyes. His heart lodged in his throat.

"You were never my second choice."

The desire to kiss her burned straight through him as if he were parchment paper lost for decades. He cupped her face. Her skin was cool against his heated touch. She leaned into him. Her soft breasts pressed against his chest. The tip of her tongue darted out over her lips. An ocean roared in his head, blocking out all logic. He brought his lips to hers because he could not contain the desire to feel her.

She yielded her mouth to his. As their tongues met, a deep ache settled over his body. He wanted her more than he wanted anything else. She wrapped her arms around his neck, pulling him closer. He kissed her deeper, remembering every inch of her mouth and memorizing all the new ways she set him on fire.

"What in tarnation is going on here?"

They jumped apart, as if the intrusion caused a misfire. It had for him.

Huck Wilde stood on the porch in his sweater and corduroy pants. His face was a deep red. The back of his hair stood at attention, as if he'd been lying on it. His eyes burned with a fierceness. There was nothing sleeping about this guy. In fact, if this wasn't New Jersey, Ford was certain the man would be wielding a shotgun.

"Nothing, Dad. Go back inside." Nyx wrapped the blanket around her.

"Hello, Mr. Wilde. Nice to see you again." Heat climbed into his cheeks. He might as well be sixteen again.

"You're that McKay boy, aren't you?" Huck narrowed his bushy eyebrows.

"Yes, sir." He didn't bother to say he wasn't a boy but a grown man, considering he was about to ravish his daughter's mouth on Huck's front porch.

"The high school principal?"

"That's right."

"Do you teach your students to disgrace themselves on their parents' front porch at all hours?" Huck crossed his arms over his still sizeable chest. All the men in Nyx's family were built like the side of a barn. Well, most of them — her father, a couple of her uncles, and her cousin Brad. In high school, he and Brad got along fine, although they didn't run in the same crowd, but Ford never wanted to cross Brad. He wondered if Brad had ever chased away any of his sister's boyfriends. Ford was glad Brad was only a cousin right now and not a brother. Huck was someone Ford could handle, if it came to it, which he hoped beyond hope it would not.

"No, sir."

Nyx arched a brow and smirked at him. She must be loving this inquisition.

"Give it a rest, Dad. I'm a grown woman. No one is ruining my reputation. I did that just fine by myself."

He wondered exactly what she meant by that. They had been each other's firsts. Her reputation had been completely intact back then. He hadn't told a soul they did it. Unless she was referring to her recent episode on stage, but she had nothing to be embarrassed by. He wished she knew that.

"I should go." He gripped her elbow. She looked at him.

"No," Nyx said.

"Good idea." Huck waved his arm toward the steps.

"Dad, go inside and mind your own business. Ford and I weren't doing anything wrong."

Huck huffed and went inside. The door closed with a loud bang.

"Your father still doesn't like me."

"He doesn't like anyone. I'm not sure he likes me. Don't take that grand display personally."

"As a father of a daughter, I can tell with certainty that your father loves you. He came out here to protect you."

"I don't need protecting."

"Doesn't matter. Delaney might only be nine, but I'm pretty sure that when she's our age, I will still want to leap in front of any runaway trains."

She leaned into him again. "Are you a runaway train?"

"Is that what you're looking for?" He had often tried to tether her to the ground so she wouldn't fly away on some crazy idea.

"Do you want to go into the woods with a few beers?"

"Like when we were kids?"

"Exactly like that."

"We can go into a bar and drink now. And if you're looking for what we used to do after, I have a perfectly good bed for that. Also an empty house." His words shocked him. He hadn't planned to say any of that.

She didn't flinch. She stared up at him. He held his breath.

"Let me get my coat."

CHAPTER THIRTEEN

Nyx couldn't back out now. Her mouth always got her in trouble. She had never learned that lesson —not completely. She stood in her room, with her coat in her hand, wondering if she could go through with it. She hadn't had sex in ages. She and Miles never seemed to have the time or one of them was always too tired with their busy schedules. Sleeping with Ford didn't have to mean anything except a good night. No one had to talk. Even if the sex wasn't any good, it was better than no sex.

The last time she and Ford did it, they were eighteen. It wasn't perfect or even romantic. They went into the woods, he had a blanket, and they managed as young people often do. Hopefully, she improved some with age. Hopefully, he had too.

She didn't normally shy away from a challenge and this was what it was. They were playing chicken to see who would blanch first. It wasn't going to be her. He had started this whole thing by showing up.

She hurried from her room and locked the front door behind her. Huck was nowhere in sight. He probably went to bed. He would have something to say when she returned, if he heard her coming in, but too damn bad. He was not her keeper any longer.

Ford waited for her by his car. He could still turn her belly to mush. His long legs were crossed. He stared at his phone, but his chest was well defined in his jacket he kept open. Leaning into him earlier had awakened her senses. Even the noise in her ears had calmed. His presence reassured her that life could be handled. That had been something missing from her world.

"Ready?" she said.

He looked up at her. "I am, if you are."

"Never more." She slid into the passenger side.

They drove in silence. He kept the radio off, and she was grateful for that. She didn't want one of her songs to come on, reminding them of how their lives had separated or the hurt they each felt because of it. If she thought too much about the past, she might chicken out now and that wasn't her thing. At least it wasn't before she had run off stage. She had been fearless once. Now she was nothing but a ball of fear. Maybe getting in the car with Ford, knowing full well what waited for her, was a result of freaking out in the parking lot earlier.

He pulled into the driveway of a simple one-story house with shutter-flanked windows, beige siding, and a two-car garage. The single porch light welcomed them in. The house was void of Christmas decorations, but that didn't take away from its charm. Though she wondered if their absence was because he hadn't found the time or was soured by life and the holiday season. He didn't love his job no matter what he said. His eyes had told a different story than his few words had.

In the dark, it was hard to tell where his property stretched, but since it was Candlewood Falls, she could assume he was on at least an acre. The quaint house with boxwood bushes and a black mailbox by the road was exactly the kind of house she had pictured for him.

He hurried around the car to open her door, but she scooted out before he could get there. This wasn't a date. Just two people who were attracted to each other, a hookup without some of the danger.

"Are you sure about this?" He held her gaze.

She could get lost in the warm brown of his eyes. He was her opposite in every way, from their eye color to the way they approached life, but that had never stopped her from falling for him. He had been the tether to her soul once. She had hoped that she could be the wind beneath him, but he had never let go long enough to try.

"Are you?" She couldn't promise him anything. "This is a one-time deal, Ford. No lifetime commitments. I can't give you that. We might even regret it the minute it's over."

"Jeez, I hope not. Look, I'm not asking you for forever. I'm not that kid anymore."

She hoped so. She also hoped she wasn't the young woman who had wanted a life with this man, because if she was, she might ask him to follow her again. "Will you still want Delaney to have singing lessons?" She didn't want anything to get in the way of that. Delaney needed the support and shouldn't be a victim of their decisions.

"She has nothing to do with this. Right here, right now is about us and some unfinished business."

She had plenty of that these days. "It sounds like we've come to an agreement."

He took her hand and led her inside.

She had thought about this moment many times, wondering if it would even happen. Ford left most of the lights off. The shadowed rooms offered cover from misunderstood facial expressions and body language. The darkness softened the stark reality they were probably making a giant mistake but couldn't seem to stop themselves. She had envisioned more urgency. Instead, there was a calmness as if a warm blanket protected them. She expected awkwardness or rushing, not this familiarity with time to spare.

A single table lamp lit the corner of the living room. It cast enough of a soft glow for her to see this room was lived in, as it should be. Remotes were strewn on the coffee table along with a box of crayons, some of the colors sprinkled around, blank paper, and several rolls of colored duct tape. A pink blanket was bunched on the corner of the couch with its well-worn cushions.

She was intruding on Ford's comfortable life. This was a mistake. She should go.

"Do you like beer?" He stood in the kitchen doorway beyond the completely dark dining room with heavy furniture.

If the noise in her head had been any louder, she may have missed what he said, but the powers that be gave her a saving grace tonight after the disaster at the mall. If she focused, she could hear almost a whistle in her ear, but if she allowed herself to forget she had tinnitus, it was as if it granted her some peace.

She hesitated. Go or stay?

"Nyx, can you hear me?" He stepped closer, smiling. His eyes always crinkled when he smiled with deliberation. He was an incredibly handsome man with his broad shoulders and narrow waist. He wasn't a gym guy with bulky muscles, but those muscles were there and she wanted to feel each and every one of them.

"Ford, can we skip the beer?" Her pulse quickened as if she had come to the end of a rock ballad where she would belt out the final lyrics.

"No beer?" He arched a brow.

She cleared the space between them so they were cloaked by the absence of light in the dining room. She ran her hands up his strong and defined chest and onto his shoulders.

"If we stop for a drink, I might change my mind."

"It's okay to change your mind. There's no pressure here."

Of course, there wasn't. He was always the gentleman. He would never force her to do anything she didn't want to. He didn't even try to force her to stay or force her to leave her first fiancé when she called and told Ford her news. He had been silent on the other end of that long-distance call. She had regretted her decision to phone him. He had congratulated her with a thickness in his voice she still heard all these years later. He had rushed off the phone with some excuse and they never spoke again—until she bumped into him outside of Green Bean.

"I'm sorry I hurt you in the past." She needed to clear some of the air.

"Let's not talk about the past, okay? I don't want to dig up old stuff. I want to take you to bed and make love to you because it's all I can think about. I don't want to worry about what will happen after that either."

The sound of that proposition heated her core. She preferred no promises, no hurt feelings. The just now. "Will you show me your bedroom?"

He led her down a hallway off to the left where three bedrooms waited. His was at the end of the hall and the biggest of the three with its own bath.

The room suited Ford with its large bed and leather headboard. A mural of trees done in grays and blacks highlighted the wall behind the bed.

The curtains were pulled back from the floor-to-ceiling windows that looked out onto the back of the house. A small round table and a chair sat in front of the window. Must be a nice view when the sun hung high in the sky. She could picture him having coffee in the morning, sitting there contemplating his day or even his life.

Wood planks and black beams made up the ceiling. Glass teardrop lamps hung from the ceiling as it cried its light down on the bed.

"Too much?" Ford dimmed the overhead light, muting everything.

"This room is beautiful. You have some eye."

"My mother sent her interior designer over when I bought the house. She wanted me to have a masculine space in case, you know, something like this happened." He offered her a sheepish grin.

"Golda wanted that for you?" She couldn't imagine either of her parents being so straightforward.

"She was very glad to see Tenna go. She thought a new room would inspire me."

Nyx slid up to him and ran her hands over his hips, settling them in his back pockets. She was glad Tenna was out of the picture too. "So, how many times have you showed off this room?"

He pressed against her, wrapping his arms around her waist. "That is none of your business." He winked.

"Ah. Many. You're some kind of a stud." Women would be foolish not to grab Ford for themselves. He came from a wealthy family, even if his father was a snob. Ford had a good work ethic. He may not be working at his dream job, but she didn't doubt his abilities. His biggest problem had been that he never trusted himself. He probably still didn't.

"Never mind how many women I've been with or I'll start asking you for a number."

"Three." She didn't hesitate, wasn't ashamed.

"Three? That's it? You're one of the most popular female singers in your genre. Hell, in music. You haven't taken advantage of the men who must have thrown themselves at you?"

His words shocked her. What other assumptions had he made over the years? What was she doing here in his bedroom only days after returning home? This behavior was just like her, always jumping without thinking. She and her sister had that in common, but Nyx had taken it to another level. Her music career was proof of her impulsive choices. She was grateful it had all worked out. But now? With her heart on the line again?

She slipped out of his grasp and sank onto the corner of the bed. "Is that what you think? That I slept around because I had willing participants." She had many men and a number of women proposition her. Some were legitimate offers, people wanting to get to know her first, and others were simply groupies. None of it appealed to her. She had wanted someone who was there for her and not her career and what it offered. The typical issue for anyone with celebrity. A hazard of getting what she wanted.

"I just meant... sorry. I don't know what I meant." He scratched the back of his neck.

"I think you do. You seem to think that I live this wild and crazy life in the music world. That I don't have the values I left town with because I was engaged twice or because you believe every tabloid who posts something about me. Is that it?"

"Nyx, I don't want to argue with you."

"Why not, Ford? Because it requires you to feel something unpleasant?" She reached for the words she tossed out, but they were out of her grasp and hitting him full force. He flinched.

"You know what. I think we should call it a night."

"That's a good idea. You don't need to give me a ride. I'll get a lift." She hurried down the hall and shrugged into her coat. She needed to get out of there before the heat of embarrassment burned her to the core.

"A car service will take hours to come here. Let me take you home. I brought you here."

"What?" She turned to face him. Some of his words were blotted out by the revving in her ear. When had that started? She shook her head as if that would set free the noise and she would be able to hear again.

"Are you okay?" He grabbed her elbow.

"I'm fine." She yanked her arm away, then turned for the door.

"Nyx, wait," he said loud enough for her to hear.

"I don't want to wait. I want to get as far from your house as I can. This was a mistake coming here." Tears burned her eyes. She fought them away.

He stepped in front of her. "Please don't say that. I'm sorry. When I'm around you…"

"Let me go. You deserve someone better than I am." She didn't need to hear about how he felt around her. She infuriated him and right now she didn't need that. Miles had made it clear how annoying her problems were.

He moved to the side, but still looked right at her. "Let me finish. When I'm around you, I want things to be the way they were, but how can that be since I haven't seen you in years. My heart doesn't understand. But my head…"

"Your head knows we're no good together. I get it. It's too late for us. Listen, my head is killing me. The ringing is on overdrive. I just want to lie down. I'll see you around." She tried to push past him, but he stood before the door.

"Give me a second, please."

"Ford, why won't you let me go? You're not turning into some creeper, are you?" She forced a laugh over her lips, but he only stared back, unamused.

"I'm not some weird guy trying to hold you against

your will. I just want to say one thing before you go. Then I'll never bother you after this."

"Okay."

"It's always been you. No one has compared. I don't know what that means for you or says about me, but in my entire adult life, I haven't felt for another woman the way I feel for you. Maybe it's the idea of you. I don't know, but I want to find out." He dropped his gaze and toed the floor.

She wanted to touch him but kept her hands at her sides. He didn't understand what she was up against with her hearing problems. She could go completely deaf someday. How would he feel about her then? She would probably never sing for an audience again. What would become of her without the only career she's ever known? If she returned to the music scene, he would stay here and run a school. She couldn't stay here. How they felt didn't matter. But if she was smart, she'd tell him that no one had compared to him ever. That was why she never set a wedding date either time. She kept waiting for him to come in and save her, love her, be with her.

"Once you got to know me, you wouldn't like what you see. Most people don't." She pushed past him and out into the cold. She closed the door behind her. The brisk air smacked against her like a coiled towel.

Leaving now before they started anything was best for both of them. She would hurt him again, and she didn't want that on her conscience. She wanted to remember Ford smiling at her with his crinkled eyes and sense of ease he carried when he wasn't paying attention. She didn't want to be the person who caused all his pain.

He deserved to be carefree. To live the life he wanted. He might want her now, but he wouldn't forever. He just didn't know it. The moment he realized she was more trouble than she was worth was the moment she would shatter.

CHAPTER FOURTEEN

F ord wanted to kick himself. He had allowed Nyx to dash out of his house upset. They had walked up to the fire with their innuendos and sexual tension, but she had backed away. He had said too much. He should've kept his mouth shut and just made love to the woman.

Now, he stood at his office window in the high school and looked out onto the parking lot filled with cars and trucks in various price ranges and levels of age. The student lot was right outside the front doors where the administrators could glance once in a while and ensure nothing out of line happened at the beginning and end of the school day. They also had the local police drive by at those times to handle the bigger issues.

He had a meeting with Meghan Turner, Jake's mother, in a few minutes. Jake was a junior who was well liked by most. Like a lot of teenagers whose life was easy with good looks and good grades and an athletic ability that worked well in high school, Jake sometimes allowed his luck to make him behave like a spoiled kid.

Jake had been accused of teasing other kids in physical education, but Mr. Reilly, the physical education teacher, couldn't make anything stick. Jake had participated in a food fight and word had it he brought alcohol to football games. Typical kid stuff. Ford reserved his opinions about Jake, but his mother... well, Ford had opinions about her.

He stayed late on a Friday to meet with Mrs. Turner because she didn't have any other time in her otherwise overwrought schedule. He didn't bother to mention he had a child of his own who needed her father's attention because he assumed his protests would fall on deaf ears. Mrs. Turner had a habit of bullying her way in to see whichever teacher had crossed her path.

Mrs. Turner's beloved son was failing English, and she had demanded to meet with Ford and the guidance counselor. Mrs. Turner had been on his radar for two years now. She had called and emailed more times than any other parent in the grade. Apparently, she had been doing that since her son was in kindergarten. Now she was Ford's issue.

He put down his coffee mug, filled with Diet Coke, and pinched the bridge of his nose. He did like his job. He had meant what he said to Nyx last night, but being the principal wasn't enough any longer. He wanted more. He wanted to direct change and protect the learning interests of the children more than he wanted to meet with parents about a seventy-five on an essay.

"Mr. McKay?" Beth, his assistant, stood in the door with a stack of files clutched to her chest. Beth was quiet, but pleasant. She kept to herself, didn't gossip with the other employees, wore her hair pulled back, no makeup on her unlined skin, and a straight skirt with a blouse as her standard uniform. The most descriptive thing on her appearance was the tiny gold cross that hung around her neck. He had tried a few times when he came on board to engage her in conversation, if only to make sure she was comfortable in her position, but she kept her answers short and did not inquire about him. He let it go. She did her job well. What else could he ask for?

"Yes?"

"Mrs. Turner is here. Do you want me to send her in now?"

"Where is Mr. Adams?" He didn't want to start this meeting without his colleague. He didn't deal with the students on a daily basis like the guidance counselors did. Mr. Adams would have an insight into Jake. Mrs. Turner had strongly suggested none of Jake's teachers be present.

"Oh, Mr. Adams had to leave. His mother fell in the Walmart in Flemington. They had to call an ambulance."

"I'm sorry to hear that. When did he leave?" He would shoot a text to Adams later and check-in. He might need a few days off if his mother wasn't well.

"About ten minutes ago. He asked if I would tell you. I was down the hall trying to find Mr. Reilly. He was having that other problem we spoke about. You know, the one with the boys and the soap. I couldn't get down here faster."

Great. The students were more riled up than usual, causing all kinds of chaos. Mr. Reilly and the soap problem was quickly becoming an issue. He'd have to talk to him too.

Now, he would have to meet with Mrs. Turner alone,

not the first time, but after last night he hadn't slept a wink. He was too pent-up thinking about Nyx running out on him. He wanted to go home to Delaney and start his weekend. He didn't have the energy for an over-bearing parent or a bunch of students who couldn't control themselves.

Beth stared at him, waiting for his response.

"Can you bring me Jake's file? And then let Mrs. Turner in." He loosened his tie. He never liked wearing ties. It might be why he had a hundred, at least. He hoped that one day he would find the perfect tie to reflect how he felt about being a teacher, then an admin-istrator, and then a principal. He still hadn't found it.

She handed him the first three files she held. Their weight bounced in his hand. Beth turned on her heel and a few minutes later, Mrs. Turner strode into his office with the confidence of three rock stars, before he had a chance to review Jake's files.

Having grown up in Candlewood Falls, he had assumed he would know all the families in his school. That had been a mistake. Plenty of families had moved in after he had left. Candlewood Falls was the kind of town people gravitated toward in order to raise their children in a safe environment with good schools and low crime.

"Thank you for seeing me, Mr. McKay." Mrs. Turner stuck out her hand. Her long fingers wrapped around his. Her skin was cold, but the shake was firm. She held his gaze with earnest. A cloud of flowered perfume hovered around her. A sneeze tickled the inside of his nose.

"That's what I'm here for." He stole a glance at the clock on the wall behind Mrs. Turner's head. He would give this woman exactly fifteen minutes, then he would end the meeting and get home. Delaney wanted to get a Christmas tree this weekend. He needed to make sure that happened for his little girl. She had too many hardships in her short life. That was another reason he would not end the singing lessons with Nyx now that they had begun. Nyx might not be right for him, but he hoped she was what Delaney needed. The problem would be when Nyx left town and went back to her regular life. He would have to make Delaney understand that Nyx would not stay.

"Why don't you have a seat?" He indicated the guest chairs in front of his desk. He dropped down into his chair and folded his hands on the desk, taking the *I'm listening* pose he practiced most of his career.

Mrs. Turner shrugged out of her camel-colored wool coat and draped it over the back of the chair. She smoothed down her hair and sat.

"I needed to talk to you about Jake's English grade. He's in AP Lang with Mrs. Lewis. Jake wrote his last paper, and it was several pages long. He always gets his homework done around all the baseball practice. He's on two travel teams. My husband and I think it's a lot, but Jake loves baseball. If he didn't love it, then we would tell him to stop."

He held up his hand to stop the rambling and save her on the time limit he had imposed and she wasn't aware of. If he had a quarter for every parent who told him their child loved playing sports and if they didn't said parent would stop the chaos, he could retire now and ditch the superintendent gig.

"Mrs. Turner, Jake is a good kid. His teachers enjoy

having him in class." Truth be told, some of his teachers found him pompous and unmotivated. He could be found scrolling on his phone instead of paying attention or participating in the classroom discussion.

"Yes, thank you. We're very proud of him."

"As you should be."

"I'll get to the point." She smoothed down her hair again. "Jake handed the paper in on time, but the teacher graded it with a seventy-five. Jake can't have a seventy-five on this paper. It's a large portion of the marking period grade and will destroy his grade point average. He's looking at some very impressive colleges. He has to get into them."

"Why is that?"

"His whole future hinges on the right college accepting him. Where will he be if he ends up some-where small with no connections? It's not as if he wants to be a teacher. If he did, then by all means he could go to a state school and call it a day. But he has bigger aspi-rations than being a teacher. Not that there's anything wrong with being a teacher. It's just not for Jake." Her hand went toward her hair again, but it changed direc-tions and returned to her lap.

"Of course not." He bit back the rest of the words bubbling up in his mouth that tried to get loose. Mrs. Turner had effectively insulted the entire education system, including him and Mrs. Lewis who had complained about Mrs. Turner more than once. She also had no idea what she was doing to her son by dictating his every choice.

"Can you change his grade?"

He hesitated, waiting for her to say she was joking,

but Mrs. Turner sat there staring at him as if he had sprouted two heads. Her overdone eye makeup blinked at him several times before she huffed an exasperated sigh. She was serious and he was amazed—though he shouldn't be. When she had requested this meeting, he had assumed she would want him to help Jake get a chance to do extra credit or an additional paper, but not to actually change the grade.

"Mrs. Turner, Jake received the grade he earned."

"I paid a tutor a lot of money to help Jake write that paper. Are you telling me I hired an incompetent tutor?"

"Sounds as if you may have. Or Jake did not take his tutor's advice. Either way, I can't change a grade one of my teachers issued. If Mrs. Lewis believes Jake's work reflects a seventy-five, then that's the decision, and I stand by it. I'm sorry you wasted your time coming in today. I have no power to change grades." He stood. If he left now, he could pick up Delaney before her singing lesson ended with Nyx. Even though things ended badly last night, he still wanted a chance to see her and maybe explain himself.

"We both know that's not true, Mr. McKay." She remained in her seat, unaffected by his movement around the office, gathering his phone and sticking it in his pocket. "You're in the perfect position to insist your employee do what you ask. Everyone has to listen to their boss."

"That's not how I run my school. My teachers are the boss in their classrooms. They know the students and they are the ones coming up with the assignments. Jake will have to live with the grade." This conversation was over. He would not continue to entertain a parent who had lost sight of what was right just to please their child who didn't deserve it.

She finally stood but leaned forward. "Mr. McKay, do you know who my husband is?"

"I'm afraid not." When he first started teaching after his master's degree, his principal at a little elementary school by the shore made it a point to know all the parents of his students along with the student's siblings if there were any. Ford was impressed with the skill, but never mastered it.

"My husband golfs every Friday with Larry Grobin most of the year. You must know Larry." Her smile slid across her face but did not reach her eyes. Her cold gaze implied anything but joy and happiness.

Oh, he knew who Larry Grobin was. Larry was on the board of education, had a strong personality nearing on aggressive in many circumstances, and had a large say in whether or not Ford would be given the superintendent's job. His application was public knowledge and something Mrs. Turner would have no problem accessing. She might've even been at the board meeting where the candidates were listed. This woman was threatening him as if they were in a television drama.

"I know Larry very well." They hadn't golfed together, but he had run into Larry many times in town.

"I thought so. I wouldn't want Larry to hear the high school principal isn't in the business of working as a team with the parents and students. Everyone wins if Jake gets a better grade. Nothing too high. I understand he doesn't deserve an A, but he's worth more than a seventy-five." She offered a conspiratorial look as if they actually were a team trying to find a way to improve

Jake's grade and not a meddling mother who had taken away her son's ability to advocate for himself or the opportunity to learn that working hard paid off and he couldn't always get what he wanted.

Ford suddenly wondered if Jake even knew his mother was in the principal's office, fighting for a better grade. If Ford had to guess, Jake was off with his baseball team, working on plays or making out with another teenager in the back seat of a car with the radio blaring, or worse, teasing some other student who didn't play sports at all, and not giving his English grade a second thought. In fact, Jake probably didn't give a second thought to which college he would attend either. Not when he had his mommy to do it all for him.

"Mrs. Turner, my apologies, but I have to cut this meeting short. I have another one across town. Thank you for coming in." He grabbed his coat. His only meeting was with Delaney and maybe a glimpse of Nyx.

"But what about my son's grade?"

He also didn't appreciate being threatened by a woman who had more connections and clout than many others and tried to use it to abuse her power. He wanted the superintendent job. It would pay him more money and that never hurt. It would open doors otherwise closed and might make him feel as if he had accomplished something with his career so he could stop thinking about regrets. Regrets that had showed their head the minute Nyx returned to Candlewood Falls.

Nyx had taken her dreams seriously. He had tucked his away in the attic.

He would not kowtow to this woman, even if he should. He might regret it later, but so be it. Another day he might've been more willing to put up with her, but after last night with Nyx and not getting enough sleep and the long day at work piled on top of the endless long days, he didn't care about the consequences.

"His grade stands. Good day."

CHAPTER FIFTEEN

Nyx pulled out her hearing aids, and the relief was like spitting out a piece of gum chewed far too long. She had finally caved and tried them. They helped the tinnitus, but she didn't want to wear them. After a few hours, they hurt her ears. They were also useless during the singing lessons. The piano vibrated in her head with each key stroke. Hearing aids weren't giving her what she wanted—her hearing back. This was a bandage fix, not the solution.

"Let's try that again," she said to Delaney.

They were in Golda's living room again. Golda had plastered her with snacks when she had arrived. Nyx had protested, but Golda wouldn't hear of it. They were practicing the song Delaney would sing at the showcase. The song wasn't hers, and it wasn't the Christmas song she had selected for Delaney.

Nyx wanted to choose something different for her than a pop song out of her young singing range, but Delaney's heart was set on this one. Nyx swallowed the lessons about song choice and vocal range and let the girl sing. She was better than Nyx had assumed based on previous lessons. At least, when she could hear her.

The tinnitus was back full force today and driving her crazy. After Ford had left last night, the motorcycle engine roared to life, taking sleep away. She had paced the floor for hours, but it never quieted down. Eventually she fell asleep from pure exhaustion and the Def Leppard album she played softly in the background. Any kind of background noise lowered the constant noise in her head.

She needed a better plan to fix her hearing problems so she could get back on the road. Luther had texted her again.

When are you coming back? He had written, *I miss my friend.*

Miss you too. That had been the truth. She missed his funny personality and his ability to like everyone no matter what. *Come to Candlewood Falls.*

I will, he had sent.

Great. When? She could pick Luther's brain for any ideas on how to rearrange the sound equipment on stage to help her, but she didn't want to do it in a text. She needed to see his face and the warmth in his eyes. He was like a favorite uncle who had the answers when no one else did. Plus, he would draw her diagrams of the stage to help her understand how he could make the sound work. If he could. Her excited mind ran ahead of her with new possibilities on returning to work.

Soon.

Hurry. I want to talk about the sound setup on stage to help my ears. Okay, she couldn't wait.

"Like this?" Delaney said, drawing her attention away from the phone.

Nyx shoved it in her back pocket. She could get back to Luther later.

Delaney broke out into song. Her entire face became a mask of emotions while she sang. Delaney scrunched up her eyes and tilted her head back so her curls floated behind her. The bow on her head slipped off, but Delaney didn't seem to notice.

Nyx remembered that kind of bliss from singing. The joy had bubbled inside her from around the age of nine and never went away. She missed singing to the crowd where the energy of thousands of people singing along could lift her right off the stage.

Delaney carried her tune in a less than perfect bucket, but she kept right on going. For a nine-year-old, she had a sense of style. It wasn't one Nyx recognized, but she loved the uniqueness. Especially the socks trimmed in pink feathers that poked out of her black combat boots. Delaney's tights were striped pink and red and she wore a long tunic sweater that came almost to her knees. Nyx couldn't get enough of her cuteness.

A cold breeze swooped in, startling her in her seat, but didn't seem to affect Delaney at all. Nyx turned in the direction of the wind and found Ford standing in the doorway, smiling at them. She checked her phone for the time. The lesson still had fifteen minutes. What was he doing there already?

Golda had assured her that he had an after-school meeting with a parent and would not make it in time. She had tried to hide the relief of not seeing him, but she wasn't sure she had pulled it off. Golda was too observant.

Delaney finished up her song and threw herself at Ford. "Daddy." He picked her up and swung her around.

Nyx ignored the clenching of her heart as if a fist had reached through her ribs and took hold with all its might. His face glowed as he stared at his child. She would not think about what it would be like to have a family with Ford. She. Would. Not. Raising children had not been her plan.

"Hey, kiddo. How was school?" He deposited Delaney on her feet. "Hello, Nyx." He offered her a stiff nod.

"Hello." She busied herself with the sheet music and putting her hearing aids in her purse before he could see them. She didn't want anyone noticing and asking questions. The devices were still new and awkward for her.

"School stunk. I don't like the other kids. They're mean to me." Delaney dropped onto the sofa and held her chin in her hands.

"How are they mean?" Ford said.

"They don't like my clothes or my bows." Delaney tugged on her tights.

"Kids can be rotten." She placed a hand on Delaney's head. Nyx had her share of unpleasantness in school. She had always been a little different too. Performing in the school musicals had never made her very popular, and being the child of one of the least liked men in town didn't make her any extra friends.

"Well, it's still early in the school year. Maybe you have to give them a chance." Ford tossed his coat on the chair. His dress shirt was wrinkled and his tie hung loose around his neck.

With a closer look, his eyes were rimmed red and dark thumbprints pressed against the skin under his eyes. Even with fatigue masking his face, he was still the most handsome man she had ever seen. But he was tired too often.

"I don't want to give them a chance. Jodi made fun of my clothes today and Beth said my bows were dumb. Then no one would play with me on the swings. When I ran over, everyone ran the other way." Delaney's chubby cheeks bloomed red and her bottom lip trembled.

"Did something else happen?" Ford sat beside his daughter.

"No. They don't like me because of the way I dress. Gregory told me I looked stupid. I told him stupid was a bad word, then he told Mrs. Applegate I said stupid."

Delaney had not mentioned any of this when Golda had asked her earlier. Nyx had been right there.

"I know what it's like to be teased. It's not any fun. If you want them to stop, you need to stand up for yourself." She squatted down to look Delaney in the eye. That move also put her closer to Ford. His thigh was only an inch away. She forced her hands to hang loose and not touch him.

"Nyx, thanks for the help, but Delaney and I have it. We can talk about this at home. Is the lesson over?"

His words stung. He didn't trust her, and she was only trying to help. "I think so. You did great." Nyx held her hand out so Delaney would high-five her.

Delaney walloped her with a lot of force, knocking her off-balance while still in her squatted position. Her feet left the floor for better pastures, but only found the air. She reached out, attempting to keep solid ground beneath her. Her hand grasped Ford's leg with urgency, but her butt still hit the floor.

His hand clasped over hers and a warm current radiated up her arm. Heat filled her face, but that had to be from the graceless landing in front of the man she wanted to appear calm and cool in front of.

"Are you okay?" Ford leaned over her. She caught a whiff of coffee and amber.

"I'm fine." She pulled her hand free and climbed to standing.

"Wow. You fell on your butt." The smile returned to Delaney's face. "I'm going to say goodbye to Lolli and Pop." And she skipped from the room, chuckling.

"I'm glad I could entertain her. At least she forgot about what had happened at school." She needed space from Ford and cleared the room to gather her belongings and her dignity.

He followed her and stood in her line of sight. "She's easily amused. And influenced. Listen, I appreciate what you were trying to do before with Delaney, giving her advice about bullies, but things are different now than when we were in school. She can't retaliate. She'll get in trouble."

"But you want her to get picked on? I don't understand." Her father had given her advice about the kids who teased and taunted. He had said to walk right up to them and stand toe-to-toe, don't back down. If they smelled weakness, they would come for blood. Bullies were like sharks. Huck didn't always give the best advice, but that one had worked and she was glad for that lesson. She would tell him that if he didn't always find a way to make her feel as if she was a failure.

"Of course, I don't. We're working on it."

"Your way doesn't appear to be working very well." She shrugged into her coat and slung her tote over her shoulder. She wanted to get out of there and go anywhere else. She was glad the date was off. She wasn't as anxious about what happened in the parking lot last night, but after their fight and the near sexual miss, it was best if she and Ford didn't pursue anything.

"I can't very well tell her to pick a fight."

"Why not?" She went toward the door, but he followed again. Ford would not be dissuaded easily. Too bad he hadn't felt that way about his music career.

"That's the rule. It's a law, in fact. I'm a school principal. How will it look if I tell her to fight back?"

"It will look like you've given your child good advice and that she can't be messed with. Look, I know my dad is not the greatest, but I have to say, Huck told each of us to stand up to the kid bullying you. When that happened, no one bothered us again."

"I've tried to tell her to ignore the kids. I'm encouraging her to be her own person and not let anyone tell her how to dress. In time, the kids will come around." He leaned in and lowered his voice, forcing her to focus harder on what he said.

"Let's take this outside." She turned toward the kitchen before opening the door. "Good night, Golda. Good night, Delaney."

Ford was quick on her heels. The cold, damp air

wrapped around her. Christmas lights twinkled in their bright-white glory, giving her the ability to see the fatigue on Ford's face. Now wasn't the time to have this conversation with him. She remembered from their time together how he would shut down or blow up when he was overwhelmed by something his father had done or an exam gone wrong. But she couldn't stop herself now that they had gone down this road.

"I realize I'm not a parent, but I do know what it's like to be different. She needs to be allowed to advocate for herself, especially if she's a quirky kid." She was an unusual kid too. Who had big, weird dreams that no one believed would come true. Her mother had been the one to pull her aside and say, *go after it, Nicole. Don't let anyone tell you no.*

"It's easier to get along than to rock the waters."

"Easier for who?"

"For her." Ford rubbed his hands up and down his arms. His breath came out in white puffs.

"For you." She poked him in the chest. His eyes flew open wide, and she instantly regretted touching him. Not because she didn't like it. Because she did. His muscles were firm under that dress shirt. He had kept in shape over the years and held up far better than she had with her long months on the road, eating whatever junk they drove past.

"Maybe. But you don't know how hard it is to be a parent, always debating if I'm making the right choice. I love her uniqueness and want her to be her own person. I do. That's why I never tell her to stop wearing the bows. But what if I'm giving her the wrong advice?

What if I should tell her to leave the bows at home so she'll fit in with the others? She and I would have one less battle to deal with." He stepped away from her and leaned against the column. He ran a hand over his face.

She wanted to reach out and make him feel better, but she doubted he wanted reassurance from her. He had already pointed out her inability to understand being a parent, but she wanted to help him, ease some of his pain.

"Anything worth doing is usually hard. You don't want her to fit in at the expense of her identity." She wasn't so sure life had done Ford a lot of favors with his divorce and his predictable career. He had always been practical, but he had a fire in his eyes once. That fire was gone, and she hoped he would get it back.

"She's nine. Her identity could change at any minute. I just don't want her being picked on at school."

"I totally agree with that sentiment. That's why I said tell her to stand up for herself and own that adorable offbeat part of herself. She shouldn't be ashamed of who she is."

"Neither should you."

"What does that mean?" Weren't they just talking about Delaney? "This whole conversation is not about me."

"Isn't it, though? You're embarrassed about your hearing. So what if you can't hear as well as you used to? You're still the same person where it counts. You're still as talented." He pushed off the column and stood inches away.

She tilted her chin to meet his gaze. "So what that I

can't hear? Is that what you're saying? This is my career that's in jeopardy. My entire life is crashing in on me like some broken-down barn out on Route 523. I'm trying to get back to my old self. Your daughter just wants to be a little girl who has fun and a way to express herself. These are not the same things."

"Maybe when you finally accept what's happened to you, you'll be able to have that very important career back."

She backed away. "My career is important. It's who I am."

"No, it's what you do."

"Performing is in my soul. I can't give it up any more than I could give up air."

He choked out a laugh. "Please spare me the drama. Are all the celebrities like this? Of course, they are. Where would they be without all the fame and fortune?"

"Is that what you think I'm about, the fame and the money? You have no idea what it's like to be hounded when all you want to do is finish a meal or go to the bathroom in peace."

"No, I don't. But you wanted that life. Don't complain now that you have it."

"I'm not complaining. I want to go back to it. I want to sing. That's all I want."

"If singing is all you want to do, you can still do it. You just might not be able to stand on a stage in a big arena with ten thousand of your closest friends screaming."

"This conversation is over. Get out of my way so I can leave." Her insides shook with fury. How dare he say those things to her, as if he knew her as well as before.

"You need to accept your life as it is."

"Like you have?"

"I'm not the one running."

"No, Ford. You're not running. You're standing completely still and letting life run by you. That's worse."

CHAPTER SIXTEEN

She should not have told Ford that he was watching his life go by. And yet, Nyx was glad she had. She had no right to judge Ford, even if he had judged her. Her stomach twisted in oily knots, thinking about the look of confusion then anger on his face when she accused him of being a bystander in his own life.

"He is, you know." She raised her wineglass to her two sisters. She lost count how many glasses she had, but she wanted to erase the memory of the pain in his eyes, pain that she had caused. That very look had haunted her for years after she left Candlewood Falls for more exciting opportunities. When he had married, she hoped that his pain was gone forever.

She hadn't wanted to hurt him back then or earlier today. He acted the way his father would concerning Delaney's problem at school, and he didn't see it. Maybe she should've said that instead.

Petra, Ember, and she sat outside at The River Winery in weathered Adirondack chairs that circled a blazing fire pit. The patio area had several spots to sit at with a small fire for each section. Only one other seating cluster had customers who dared to brave the cold night.

Outdoor heaters perched nearby, giving heat away with ease, for anyone who wanted to enjoy some wine with food on this frozen night. She and her sisters had to be crazy to be outside in December. She wasn't used to winters in Jersey anymore, but the evening offered a dry crispness like a freshly starched shirt just waiting to be worn. The moon hung pregnant in the sky amongst a spattering of stars. They each huddled in their heavy parkas, knit caps, and gloves. Petra had a blanket draped over her legs.

"You can't change Ford," Petra said.

"I don't want to change him." She did want him to see where his mistakes were. She would also like to see him in one of those starched dress shirts or better yet, out of one.

Ember arched a perfectly shaped brow. "You've been trying to change him since high school."

"I have barely seen him since high school. And back then, what did I know? He was a cute guy with a great head of hair and nice legs."

"I suspect that's not all," Petra said to Ember and held up her glass in a toast.

"That's gross coming from you." She sank back in the chair and tucked her chin inside her coat. If she could, she'd sink all the way down. Petra wasn't all that far off. Ford had the right size package. Or was the whole package. Whatever that saying was.

"You know, when I first met Mav, I thought he

163

needed a bath or was maybe a homeless guy who had stolen a really nice car."

"You did not." Ember sat up straight, her eyes wide with wonder.

"He had on ripped jeans and those tattooed arms. I never thought I was into that look. Boy, was I wrong." Petra gulped down her wine. Some of it sloshed over the side of the glass.

Petra might be a tad drunk. Ember, however, had not touched her glass at all.

Ford was far more clean-cut than Petra's Maverick. Nyx found Ford's tattoo-free skin sexy and the way he slicked back his hair so it wasn't ever in his face. He wore suits to work instead of jeans and rock t-shirts—the musicians' uniform—like every other guy she hung around. Even though she wanted him to follow his dream —even if he couldn't admit what his dream was—she wasn't sure the life of a musician on the road would fit him. It would definitely change him, bruise him, harden him.

"How are the hearing aids working out?" Ember rubbed her hands together and held them near the fire.

"I hate them." She hadn't put them back in since the singing lessons with Delaney. The ringing was a low hum at the moment. She was relaxed for the first time today. Usually alcohol made the ringing worse, but being with her sisters outside by a fire had calmed her some. When she relaxed, the tinnitus took a back seat.

She didn't want to think about it, but the noise also eased up when she was with Ford. Unless they were arguing about life's directions and the roads less traveled.

"You should wear them to get used to them," Ember said.

"I know that, smarty-pants. I don't want to wear them. They make me feel old and people treat me like I'm dumb." Ford had hit a nerve when he said she was embarrassed about her situation. He still knew her and that drove her crazy. She couldn't hide from him or herself.

"But you are not either of those things." Petra poured more wine. She held the bottle out to Ember who shook her head.

"I realize I have to keep trying. I can't wear them when I'm performing or rehearsing or producing, though. Without them, I'm struggling most days to hear the person near me. There has to be a way to diminish the tinnitus. The *just live with it* diagnosis can't be all there is." Frustration built in her chest, the way it always did when faced with this dilemma. Anger took up residence in her lungs, strangling her breath. She had to find a way, but all the information confused her, sending her in too many directions.

She stood up to have something to do with the nervous energy before her head exploded. She thought better when she moved around. At least that was what she liked to tell herself.

"I know you're having a hard time. Something will come around. You'll see," Ember said. Her sister always had the *everything will work out* attitude. She needed a little of that now.

"Will I? Will this ever get better?" She paced the small space they occupied on the patio, conscious of the other patrons watching her. She wanted her career back, but what if it was over? What was she going to do?

She didn't write her own songs any longer, not in ages. She hadn't the time with albums and touring. Studio musicians as well as musicians still trying to break into the scene sent her songs all the time. Many of them were excellent. She recorded other people's music instead of her own for a sense of ease. Could she switch to a studio musician and write music full-time? The idea scared the hell out of her. She was a performer.

"Please sit down and have another glass of wine. You're making me dizzy with all that moving back and forth." Petra poured her a generous amount of red into the glass she had abandoned when she stood.

"You're dizzy because you're drunk," Ember said.

"I thought so too." She took the glass from Petra and almost gulped it but changed her mind. She had come in her own car and had to drive home.

"I'm not drunk. Nyx, you are going to get to the bottom of your problem because you always do. Don't worry about it. The real issue is Ford," Petra said.

"No, he is not an issue. There is nothing between me and Ford to cause an issue." Well, nothing much.

"If you say so. You're too stubborn to see what is right in front of you." Petra drank the rest of her wine.

"Let's change the subject," Ember said. "How long are you staying?"

"I don't know. Through the holidays. I can't leave before the showcase. Delaney's very excited. She puts her whole heart into what she's doing. You should see her. She scrunches up her little face. Like this." She attempted to recreate the eyes squeezed shut and the chin jutting up toward the ceiling. "She waves her arms around. She's too cute."

The little girl's love of music and the innocence of not knowing what the business side was actually like made Nyx's heart swell. She could float away, watching the joy on Delaney's face.

She hadn't felt that special kind of joy in a long time. She loved what she did, but the grind tired her out more and more since her hearing had become a bigger problem. Over the past year or two, focusing and pretending everything was fine required extra energy she had to dig deep to create.

To constantly produce new material and get out there to market it, had stolen the enjoyment. That was part of the reason she had stopped writing her own music. The business side required all of her time and attention. She didn't have anything left over for her craft.

Everyone wanted a piece of her from her manager — whom she still needed to replace — to the radio outlets, internet interviewers, magazine journalists, photographers, and unfortunately, the occasional unstable fan. She had a stalker several years back that terrified her until he was caught.

Touring could age someone faster than traveling to the moon. She should be grateful that she had the chance to do what she loved every day, and she was, but sometimes the idea of a slower life had some appeal — and living near her sisters to have more nights like this one.

"You're smitten with Ford's daughter," Ember said.

"She's cute. That's all." Delaney was not someone she could get close to. Nyx knew how it worked with kids. She had plenty of friends with children who had divorced. If kids became too attached to an adult who would leave them, the children would suffer. She didn't want that kind of responsibility.

"Of course she's cute. She's Ford's daughter. But she weaved her way into your heart." Ember bounced in her seat. Her sister never could sit still.

"I hardly know her. There hasn't been time for any kind of attachment." She could deny it all she wanted, but Ember was right. Nyx adored Delaney. It had happened so quickly, she hadn't even noticed until it was too late.

"It only takes seconds," Petra said, almost reading her mind. "You could fall in love with a child at first sight."

Falling in love with Ford's daughter would rip her in two when she left town. Those singing lessons had been a mistake because now her heart was on the line.

"Enough about me and Ford. Talk about something else." There was no her and Ford. She wanted this conversation turned in another direction—any direction. She had come out tonight to forget about the argument in the driveway and the pain on his face. If she kept running it over and over, she would lose her self-control and call him.

"I have some news." Ember sat on the edge of her seat and tossed her hair behind her shoulders.

"Do tell," Petra said.

"I'm pregnant." Ember squealed and clapped her hands.

Petra dropped her wineglass, shattering it against the concrete. The wine splashed onto Nyx's jeans, making her leg cold, but she didn't care. Ember was going to have a baby.

"Crap. Look what I did. Oh, who the hell cares," Petra said, staring at the mess as if she wasn't entirely sure how it got there. "My sister is pregnant." Petra screamed and dove out of her chair. She gripped Ember in a hug.

Tears stung Nyx's eyes. Her sister would make a wonderful mother. Ember lived life without fear. Nyx had always admired that in her and emulated it every chance she could. Sometimes, taking it too far in an attempt to be her own person at the same time. As the youngest of three girls, she could feel overlooked because her big sisters were always doing things first. By the time she got around to an accomplishment, their parents had experienced it and weren't impressed.

Her mother would have been thrilled to find out another grandchild was on the way. Nyx's heart ached for what Ruby would miss.

Petra and Ember untangled themselves. Ember stared at her with expectant eyes. "What do you think, Nyxie? You haven't said a word."

She swallowed the lump in her throat. "I'm so happy for you." The tears betrayed her anyway. She gripped Ember in a big hug, not wanting to let go. All she had in this world was her sisters.

Ford's words echoed in her noisy head. Her career wasn't the only thing she had. She had these two incredible women to call sisters. She needed to stop thinking about Ford, right now.

Ember eased out of the embrace and grabbed hers and Petra's hands. "Okay, I'm excited beyond words, and

I'm terrified at the same time. Can you believe me as a mother?"

"You're going to be the best mother," Petra said.

"You have to help me. And, Nyx, you have to perform the best aunt duties."

"I promise." She held her hand up, palm out. She hadn't done a good job of being an aunt to Petra's daughter Paige. Petra never held that against her. Back then, her career was taking off and she was on the road all the time. She always made sure to send presents on birthdays and Christmas. This time around she would do a better job. Maybe she should start now with Paige.

"How is Raf feeling?" she asked.

"My handsome and sexy planner is already gathering wood to build a crib that we won't need until August. He's buying books about parenting. He says it's important he be a better father than his was."

"I'm sure he will be just fine. He's a good man." Petra continued to hold Ember's hand.

"Have you told Dad?" She wondered what her father would say about this grandchild having the last name Alvarez. Huck was not always accepting of others.

"We're telling him tomorrow. I wanted to tell you first. The only other person who knows is Brad since he's Raf's bestie. Everyone else we'll tell after the first of the year. Please keep my secret."

"You bet," she said. She didn't have anyone to share the joyous news with anyway. She might've told Miles at one time, but that wasn't going to be now.

"Do you want me to keep it from Mav and Paige? I will if you do." Petra wrapped the blanket around herself.

"Of course, you can tell them. Just no one else."

Her heart was full for Ember, but the tiniest of pricks, like a frayed guitar string poking at a finger, pierced the happiness. She had no one to build a family with. No one to come home to. Her sisters had found real love, the kind that sticks, the kind that doesn't judge the hearing loss or an empty womb. She needed to resurrect her career; otherwise, she would have nothing.

Someone squeezed her arm. She turned and Petra looked at her with pity on her face.

"I called your name three times. You didn't hear me."

She hadn't. She didn't hear her well now either. The tinnitus was back. And it's engine roared.

CHAPTER SEVENTEEN

F ord pounded another shot of tequila and banged the empty glass on the table. No one in the bar noticed. The band, a rap group turned country rockers, played loud enough to shake the walls. Of course, tonight's lineup would be a country singer. The liquor burned his throat and made his eyes water, but he didn't care. He needed to forget what Nyx said to him — because she was right.

The room tipped on its side. He gripped the table to steady himself. Maybe he had one too many. Or maybe he hadn't had enough, because he could still hear Nyx say he was watching his life go by.

He hadn't meant for that to happen. He had big plans, but never allowed them to grow because he chose the practical, safe route. Just like his father. Once Delaney was born, having a reliable career seemed like the only way to go. He had to provide for his daughter. Tenna never seemed to feel that responsibility. She walked out without a look back, needing to find herself instead of a steady paycheck.

When did he get to find himself? Probably when he retired and was too old to do anything. What would his life be like if he had hopped on that train with Nyx all those years ago? He had wrestled with that question a thousand times. Eventually, he had to shove it down so it wouldn't sideswipe him in the middle of the day. But with her back in town, looking as beautiful as ever, helping his daughter when he knew it had to kill her to do it because of her hearing issues, that unwanted thought burst free like a geyser. He needed another drink, but the waitress was nowhere to be found.

The bar was packed with young people out for a good time. He came to this bar from time to time because it was far enough away from Candlewood Falls that no one would recognize him here. The open mic night at Murphy's was a good spot when he was short on time and wanted a quick music fix.

He took a seat in the back. Here he could listen to the band play and forget for a few hours he was a school principal who used to be able to play as well as those guys on the stage.

Some nights the band called up people from the audience to jump in on a song. He hadn't seen this band before. He wasn't sure if they would do that. Those other times, he sat in his seat trying to talk himself into volunteering. He never did. He was out of practice and didn't want to make a fool of himself.

Nyx's words swirled in his head right along with the tequila buzz. She had looked right into his soul and called him out on the very thing he lived in denial about. She understood him in ways no one had—ever. He had no idea how that was possible, except the worst thing that could be true was. They did have a connection and it had never broken.

He waved the waitress over. "Can I get another, please?"

"Sure thing." She leaned in to make herself heard.

Nyx would have a terrible time in here with the band and the voices competing. He couldn't imagine what she was going through. She might be struggling with her situation, but who wouldn't? She was on top of her game and her world crashed around her through no fault of her own. He should've been more sensitive to that, but sensitivity wasn't his best quality. Instead, he had pointed out how she didn't appreciate anything.

The waitress returned with his drink. He paid for it and had it down his throat before she could wiggle between the tables and into the abyss of young people with their lives ahead of them.

The band wrapped up a song. The crowd burst into applause.

"Okay, guys, we're going to do something different for us, but we hear you all like to do this." The singer who doubled as the lead guitarist brushed his long stringy hair away from both sides of his face. He had a scraggly beard and wore a faded flannel shirt over jeans that had seen better days. The singer reminded Ford of the old grunge bands from the nineties.

The crowd went crazy again. Everyone knew what was coming. He sure did. And this time he wouldn't sit back and watch.

The singer raised his hand to quiet the crowd some.

"We're looking for someone to come on up and jam with us. One song—"

"Me. I'll do it." He jumped out of his seat before he could change his mind or anyone else could stick their hand in the air. People in the audience turned in his direction. Some wore masks of confusion. Others wore disgust as if to say who was this old guy in a wrinkled dress shirt and suit pants?

"Looks like we've got an eager beaver. Come on up, man. Let's see what you've got."

The drummer gave him a roll, and the crowd responded with a tepid applause. Sweat broke out on his body. The room tipped again as the tequila sloshed in his stomach. This was a mistake, but there was no getting out of it now. He had to hope his fingers were nimble enough to move over the fret and his voice wouldn't crack under pressure.

He weaved around the tables. A couple of people smacked him on the back as he passed to wish him luck, as if they understood how much he needed it. He stepped onto the stage with his heart in overdrive. The lights pointing at them, blinded him. The crowd became nothing more than the edges of a camera flash that wouldn't go away.

"What's your name?" The singer patted him on the shoulder, turning his attention away from the lights and saving his vision.

"Ford."

"Like the car?"

"Just like that." Not like that at all, but this wasn't the place to spill about Ford being a family name. He had that much sense at least.

"Well, Ford, I'm David."

"Hi, David."

"Let's give Ford a big round of applause, everybody."

The crowd did as instructed. He gave a wave and what he hoped was a confident smile. It still wasn't too late. He could bolt for the door. Sure, they would all laugh at him, but he didn't know any of these people. He would just never come back. There had to be other places like this one. New Jersey was the most densely populated state. Bars had to be on almost every corner in the overcrowded areas.

"What do you play?" David asked, derailing any plans of running.

"Guitar." If picking it up once every six months counted.

"Borrow mine." He slipped out of his Les Paul and handed it over.

The weight of the guitar was foreign to him. He played a Gibson. The guy was shorter too, no bigger than five-nine. The strap put the guitar too high on Ford's abdomen. It would have to do. He didn't have the dexterity or the time to fix it. Everyone was watching. "Thanks."

"What song are you going to dazzle us with?"

He hadn't thought that far ahead. He hadn't thought at all. That was the problem. He weighed out all the pros and cons of every big decision. And standing on the stage to perform in front of people was a big decision. He hadn't done this since he was in college. He wiped his sweaty palms on his pants.

"Do you know "Bringin' On the Heartbreak" by Def Leppard?" The words came out in a strangled croak. He had to swallow twice to get his saliva working again.

That was his favorite song growing up. He listened to that album on repeat for hours, driving his parents nuts. His little high school band would open with that to get the crowd revved up. Nyx would be in the front row belting out the song right along with him and giving him her giant smile that she shared with no one else. He had felt like a rock god back then.

"Hell, yes. We love Def Leppard. You mind if I sing along since you've got my gear?"

"Sure." He didn't trust himself to say much more, let alone sing.

He stole a glance at the other band members who looked back in anticipation. No one moved. The crowd grew quiet. His brain raced to catch up. Something was wrong and he didn't know what it was. Why wasn't the band playing? The drummer nodded to him and held up his sticks.

His drunk brain kicked into gear, finally. The song began with the guitar and the drums. They were waiting for him to start the damn song. Except his fingers wouldn't follow the commands from his brain. He needed to play the chords first and the drums would follow. His thick fingers fumbled on the fret. He didn't have a pick to make the right sound on the strings. His fingers slipped off, causing feedback. Someone gasped in the audience.

"Hey, no worries. We all get a little nervous," David said. "Let's try again."

He swallowed hard. He placed his fingers over the right spots on the neck. He could do this, except he couldn't remember the song. His mind betrayed him and sent every thought flying. He was left with an empty head.

"Get that loser off the stage," someone shouted.

The audience jeered in agreement. The band looked on with pity and loathing.

"Let me try," some guy said, walking up to the stage. He wore a white baseball cap and a black t-shirt. He was probably a good ten years older than Ford was. Someone who also grew up jamming to Def Leppard right from their beginning.

David held out his hand.

He had to admit defeat and hand over the guitar.

White cap guy jumped onto the stage and held his arms up as if in victory. The crowd went nuts, liking him instantly.

Ford held his head high, but he wanted to slink back, hiding. He was a pathetic excuse for a man. He grabbed his coat and pushed out into the night. The cold air sobered him up some. He gulped the air in, trying to slow his heart.

He had no business driving and had no one to call. He couldn't tell anyone what happened. No one would understand. No one except Nyx.

Nyx climbed into bed and pulled the covers up to her chin. The night with her sisters had been great, but she was cold and tired. They had stayed until the winery had closed. After a while the fire and the heaters weren't enough to keep her warm. The damp air had seeped into the parts of her that weren't covered by her coat, freezing her.

One of the best things about tonight, apart from Ember's pregnancy news, was Nyx was able to see the space for the showcase. Weezer River, the matriarch of the River family who owned the winery, gave her a tour. Weezer never changed with her helmet-style hair and her casual attire. She planned on setting up the seating and stage area much the way she had in the past. Nyx wasn't sure, but Weezer seemed a little too pleased that Uncle Silas' hotel was out of commission.

Nyx was familiar with the room for the showcase as she had been in that show and had come home several times over the years to visit. She loved the Christmas Showcase.

Delaney would need a microphone. She didn't have the lung capacity to belt out her song for the people in the back. They would also need a music track piped in to accompany Delaney. Nyx had shot off a text to Luther, asking for some help. He had immediately replied with yes in all caps. Couldn't hurt to give Delaney a tiny edge. This wasn't a competition or anything, but Nyx could pull a few strings to make a little girl's dream sparkle more.

With that taken care of, all she wanted was a good night's sleep. Tomorrow she would find a way to deal with her hearing and her career.

Her phone lit up beside her on the table. The ringtone sounded off in the distance. At least she could still hear it. For now.

Ford's name was on her screen. He had sent a text. She debated looking at it. Whatever it was could wait.

He probably wanted to reschedule Delaney's lesson tomorrow or yell at her again. Either way, she didn't want to talk to him now.

Her phone lit up again. Ford would not be dissuaded. Better to look and get it over with. She could give him a quick response and get some sleep.

Sorry to bother you. I need some help.

Please, Nicole. It's important.

It must be serious if he used her real name.

What do you need? she sent back.

He replied immediately. *A ride.*

Did your car die? She could tell him to call a taxi or a ride service. They did exist in this state even if they didn't come to Candlewood Falls all that often.

Drunk.

She stared at the screen for a minute. He was drunk and asking for a ride? She didn't understand why he wanted her help. He must have a ton of people he could call.

Why me?

Please. I'll tell you when I see you. I promise.

Her brain jumped up and down and yelled don't do it. But her stupid heart threw her legs over the side of the bed and shoved her feet into her boots.

Where are you?

He texted her the address. He was forty-five minutes away. She had expected him to say Murphy's or the new brewery on the outskirts of town, not some bar in another county. She let out a big sigh. She couldn't exactly say no now.

You owe me, she sent.

Name it.

I will. See you soon.

She went downstairs and grabbed her coat from the hook by the door. Her father was at the kitchen table with a book and a mug of tea in front of him. Only the light above the table was on, throwing most of the kitchen into shadows. The plastic gingham tablecloth shined in the lamp's effervescence.

"I didn't know you were still up." She shrugged into her coat.

"Can't sleep. Where you headed?"

"Ford needs a ride." She grabbed her purse.

"Is it safe for you to drive now?" He arched a brow.

"As opposed to?" She didn't need a lecture now about her inability to do things because she was hearing impaired.

"You know what I mean." He turned in his seat to face her. The old wood complained under his weight.

"I am a good driver. You don't have to worry if that's what it is you're doing." She had no idea if he worried about her or not. That had been her mother's department.

Huck shook his head and closed his book. "Are you back together with Ford McKay now?" He also ignored her comment about caring.

"No." Even if she was, she would hesitate to share that information with him. He would tell her all the reasons why he opposed it. He didn't like any of the men she had brought home.

"Good. I don't understand why my daughters pick the wrong men. Don't be like your sisters." He gripped the small teacup in his big, gnarled hand.

The dainty porcelain cups with their pink flowers

were her mother's. His hard worked hands, the hands of a farmer, looked wrong against the gentle cup.

"Ember and Petra have good men." The kind of man she would like to have someday. A man like Ford who could be counted on to handle his responsibilities and stand up for her when she needed it. She pushed the thoughts away. She and Ford were not going to be a thing. He was just drunk and probably not in his right mind.

"Now they do."

"You like Raf?" She didn't see that coming.

Her father waved her words away. "Ah, that Alvarez is a giant pain in the ass, but he's all right otherwise. Ember seems to love him, and he's good to her."

"Did I hear you right? My ears don't work well anymore." She jiggled her ear to add to the sarcasm.

"Stop that nonsense. I've known Alvarez most of his life."

"But he's Spanish. You know, from Spain." Her father didn't like anyone who was different from him. That ruled out a lot of people, pretty much anyone without the last name Wilde.

"He's from Candlewood Falls like the rest of us."

"And you like Maverick too? He's not from town."

"The chef? Ah. Too many tattoos. He's sloppy with his hair like my nephew. But he can cook. I'll give him that much. Petra seems happy with him, and he's good to my Paige. If he wasn't, that would be a different story."

She couldn't believe what she was hearing. Her father had definitely softened since losing his wife. Maybe he wouldn't freak out when he found out Ember and Raf were expecting. He might even be happy for them. Huck loved Paige in a way that Nyx and her sisters never experienced.

"So, why don't you like Ford? He's from town. His family has money. He has a steady job."

"That young man never knew himself. He's not confident enough for you. He'll hold you back. Don't get involved with him."

She flinched at Huck's observation. "I didn't realize you knew Ford well." If she had to guess, they didn't run in any of the same circles.

"I find things out about anyone bothering with my girls." He pushed out of the chair and poured more hot water into her mother's cup. "Your mother never liked my snooping around when one of you brought a boy home. She told me to mind my business. I told her you three were my business."

She edged up to the idea that her father had worried all along as if it were a jagged cliff with rocks below. One wrong step, and she would tumble to her death. Giving over her scarred heart could end badly. He didn't handle love with care.

"Are you saying you think he's not good enough for me?"

"He was never good enough for you, Nicole. None of those boys were good enough."

"Is that why you never liked anyone I brought around here?" She had missed that possibility until now. She wasn't sure why tonight made any difference, but hearing him say those nice things about Raf and Mav shifted her view a little.

One more realization dawned on her. Her father had faced her during the entire conversation, even when he poured more water. He didn't turn his back or talk over his shoulder. She gripped the counter to steady herself.

"What if I like Ford? Would you accept him?" She didn't know why she asked that, but she had to know.

"Ah." He waved the air again. "You and your sisters will be the death of me. Do what you want. You always do."

"Just like you."

"Too much like me. Don't be like me. Be like your momma." A small smile slipped over his lips. He had loved Ruby in ways she and her sisters hadn't understood until their mom became sick. Her mother always knew, though.

"Do you miss her?" She treaded into unsafe territory with that question. Huck wasn't one to talk about his feelings. He preferred subjects like the rainy season and apple rot. He would either yell at her or shut down completely.

"Every day." He kept his gaze on the cup, but she could hear him.

His shoulders slumped. It seemed as if the weight of losing his lifetime companion pushed him down. Life hadn't always been easy for Huck. Even if he was often the cause of his problems. Her heart softened some. For the first time, her father wasn't a giant with an angry streak and an iron fist. He was an old man, broken-hearted and alone.

The space between them filled with an awkwardness that was always their dance. They never knew what to say to each other, and she didn't know how to offer him any comfort. Petra was always better at that.

"Yeah, I miss her too." Missing her mother snuck up

on her at all hours, when she battled the fight to get her hearing back, when she stood on stage. Or at random times. When she threw in a load of laundry and the detergent smelled like her mother, or when the hydrangeas were in bloom, or like now.

"You should go. Your man is waiting."

"He's just a friend." That was all.

"Drive safely." He smiled at her. She wanted to believe that his comment meant more than what was on the surface.

"Thanks, Dad." Hers did.

CHAPTER EIGHTEEN

Nyx turned into the parking lot of the Horse and Coach Bar. Cars filled every space. Must be a popular location. She had no idea why Ford was all the way out here, but she would find out why and why he had dragged her out of bed instead of someone else.

Ford sat on the sidewalk at the corner of the building. His knees were bent and his head was in his hands. His wool coat draped his sides and pooled on the ground, hopefully not in a puddle. He looked up as she approached. When he stood, he stumbled. Definitely tipsy.

She rolled down the window on the passenger side. "You need any help getting in?"

He shook his head, then folded himself into the seat with a groan. He smelled like booze and sweat. His long legs took up most of the room between the seat and the dashboard. She soaked in his tall, thin frame. She loved the way his clothes clung to him, showing off his muscles. His coat blocked some of that view tonight, but she had plenty of memories stored away for safekeeping.

"You can push the seat back if you need to."

He did just that and leaned his head back against the headrest, closing his eyes. "Thank you for coming all the way out here so late. I didn't have anyone else to call."

"You don't have some kind of bro friend you've done this for?" She eased the car back onto the road.

"Who has time for friends?"

"I can understand that." Other than her sisters, she didn't have any real female friends. She had plenty of work acquaintances, but in her business, real people were often hard to find, and she hadn't spent the necessary time to build too many friendships. Luther might be it. She trusted the guys in her band, her roadies, and her staff. That hadn't worked out well when she considered Miles.

"Where's Delaney?"

"At my parents' for the night."

"That's good. She shouldn't see you too drunk to drive." She took the on-ramp for 287 North and merged into the high-speed traffic New Jersey was known for. She didn't miss driving on the major highways here.

He glanced at her. "I agree. I'm trying to set an example for my child and tonight was not my best night. I'm glad she's at her grandparents'."

"Why were you all the way out here?"

"Would it be okay if we drove in silence for a while? My head hurts." He pinched the bridge of his nose.

No talking would be easier for her for so many reasons. Having him this close threw her brain into a frenzy. She didn't want to like him, but she did. She always had. She could never shake him loose.

"You do owe me an explanation, and I expect to hear it. I was already warm and cozy in bed when you sent that text. I could've told you to go scratch." She should have too. It was too late to go asking for help from her. And yet she ran like a lovesick girl, the first chance she had to see him.

"You could have. Thank you for rescuing me. I swear I'll tell you everything when we get to my place. I just need some time. It's been a horrible night."

"Fair enough." She did wonder what had happened that had him too drunk to drive and calling her. It must have been a big deal.

"What were you wearing?"

"Excuse me?" She stole a quick glance at him. She wasn't sure she had heard him correctly.

His smile set off the crinkles around his eyes. He had no right to be so damn cute when he smiled.

"When you were in bed and I texted. What were you wearing?" He shifted in the seat until he was at his full height. He took up so much space that he sucked the air from her lungs.

"None of your business." She kept her gaze on the road.

"It was sexy, wasn't it?" He practically panted as if he were a puppy.

It was the exact opposite of sexy. She would not tell him that. "I thought you didn't want to talk."

"Not about what happened at the bar. I'll tell you that later. But you could distract me from my awful experience by describing your sleepwear."

"Forget it, McKay. You'll have to use your imagination." She was still in the clothes she went to bed in, her sweatpants and t-shirt. Nothing fancy. In fact, the sweatpants were so old they were falling apart, but they were worn in and comfortable in that way only used fleece could be.

"You're not any fun."

"I'm a lot of fun. You're the drunk one who can't hold his liquor. That's not fun."

He stared at her. "I don't know what's wrong with me lately."

"I was just kidding about the drunk stuff. I'm not judging you. You're a good guy. You just had a bad night."

"Ford, the good guy. That's all I ever was to you, right? Do women find the good guy hot at all?"

This conversation was quickly headed down a path she should not take. Telling him how sexy she thought he was because he wasn't one of the jerks would only get her into trouble. She had no plans to stick around after the holidays. If they explored more than that kiss from earlier, both their hearts would break.

"I think you're right. We should stop talking until we get to your house."

"If that's how you want it. You're the driver."

"It's how I want it."

"I'll stop talking."

"Thank you."

They drove the rest of the way in silence. Silence except for the ringing in her ears. Ford fell asleep by the time they merged onto Route 22. She had to shake him awake when they parked outside his house.

"We're here?" He blinked and looked around as if he couldn't remember even being in the car.

"It's your stop, hotshot." She no longer wanted to hear his explanation. She was tired. The ringing was annoying. If she could get some good sleep, she might feel better in the morning. She wanted him to get out of the car and go about his life.

"Come inside."

"I can't. It's late." She would not play with fire.

"Thanks for the ride." He opened the door and unfolded out of the seat. He took a step and fell down.

"Oh, shit." She hopped out of the car and ran around to help him. He was already climbing to his feet.

"I'm good." He held his hands up to stop her.

"You're still drunk. I'll help you inside and get you settled." She looped his arm around her shoulder. She only came up to his chest. He could take them both down without much trouble, but he stayed upright.

"I can manage." He stumbled.

"Jeez, Ford. When did you become such a lightweight?"

"I had a lot of tequila."

"That explains it. Give me your keys."

He dug around in a pocket and handed them over. They half stumbled, half walked to the door. She found the right key, then helped him inside and down onto the couch. He worked his way out of his coat.

She grabbed a glass and filled it with water. "Drink this. Do you have any ibuprofen? You're going to need it."

"In the cabinet by the kitchen sink."

She rummaged around the cabinet until she found what she was looking for. She shook out two and made him swallow them. "You good now?"

"I think so. Thank you for everything. I wasn't sure if you'd come for me."

"Why? I'm a nice person." She wanted to see him and make sure he was safe. She also liked that he had called her.

"Of course you're nice. I saw what you did for that children's hospital last year. You have a big heart. I didn't think you'd come for me because of our history."

"We were a long time ago." She wasn't sure about the size of her heart. She protected it. Helping a children's hospital was easy. Seeing the sick kids had been rough, but they had the best attitudes. Those kids were brave. She had been moved beyond words in that moment and had spent the day laughing with them and singing with them.

But when it came to men, her heart had always been closed. Every relationship after Ford had been doomed from the start. The truth was she had never given her whole heart over to anyone because Ford had it.

"But I kissed you today. Well, it's yesterday now." He checked his watch.

"Let's not discuss the kiss. I should go." The best thing to do was walk away as quickly as she could. Bringing the memory of the kiss to the forefront of her mind would only make her want to kiss him more.

"Are you sorry we kissed?"

How did she answer that? If she said yes, it would sound mean and hurtful and it would be a lie. If she said no, it would tell too much of how she felt for a man she couldn't have because their lives were so different. She really was too much like her father, playing her emotions close.

"I don't think now is the time to get into this. You won't even remember the conversation in the morning and you might want to have it again." They weren't right for each other, wanting goals at opposite ends of life's spectrum. They couldn't build a life without a similar foundation. Love wasn't always enough. It didn't have the power to keep them together before. Why would it work now?

"I'll remember tonight. I'm not that drunk."

"I doubt that."

"I remember everything, Nicole. Every single thing that involved you. That's always been my problem. From the moment I saw you in the high school hall, you were the one. I fell head over heels for you, and I haven't been standing right since."

"Ford, please." Tears burned her eyes. She couldn't think about those days when they still had every possible opportunity. Life had changed them.

He had a child who needed stability. Nyx wasn't ready to be a stand-in mother. She wanted to be on the road, singing songs she wrote. She wanted to hear those songs loud in her head as the audience screamed and clapped and sang along. She wanted every note to vibrate in her soul, bringing her to her knees with its power. Ford wanted a quiet life with a wraparound porch for watching the sun fade into the horizon, children's laughter floating across a field of green, and the rustle of the leaves in the distance playing with the wind. Sounds she may never hear again.

"I want you to know what you mean to me. You're the reason my marriage broke up." He stood and swayed a little.

She reached out to steady him. He gripped her elbows and smiled that damn smile again. The heat of his hands shot up her arms and seared her heart. She was pathetic, responding to him the way she did. It was like they were in high school when her emotions were always out of control, and she couldn't keep her hands off him.

"I didn't break up your marriage." She didn't want that responsibility put on her. She had enough of her own mistakes to carry. She didn't need to carry his too.

"Not literally. My ex-wife and I did that. But you were always the elephant in the room. Tenna knew it. Accused me of it over and over. I tried to deny it, but she was right. That was the only thing she was right about, but she was right. I have always loved you, and now you're here, standing in my living room the way I had hoped for years."

Her insides ached. Fear held her back. He was drunk and not in his right mind, but alcohol also made lips loose. There might be an ounce of truth to what he said. She didn't want to get too close to that truth in case it electrocuted her.

"I gave you a ride home and helped you inside before you fell on your face. That's why I'm standing in your living room." She tried to make light of his statement, hoping to distract him.

"It's more than that. It always has been. Please tell me. Do you feel any of the way I do?"

She didn't know how to answer. Did she walk up to the truth and shake hands with it, or did she pretend that her confused emotions hadn't hijacked her sensibility since she bumped into him on the sidewalk the other day.

"If you feel the way I do, stay the night. And if you don't, I'll let you go and never bring it up again. But I think you feel it too." He leaned his forehead against hers. His breath was warm against her face.

She put her hand on his cheek. His day-old beard scratched her fingertips. He smiled and her heart broke into a thousand pieces that she would never be able to glue back together. She loved him. She always had. She wanted to make love with him and that would end her. Once they were together, she would struggle to walk away. She couldn't have it all. No one could. A piece of her would stay in Candlewood Falls with him. Risking her heart—and his—that way was dangerous.

He leaned down and kissed her. She should stop him, but she did not want to. She wanted that kiss the way the sea wanted to touch the sand. His tongue swept her mouth, and her head spun. He tasted like tequila, spicy and hot. Her fingers curled in his soft hair. He put a hand on her low back and pulled her against him, his arousal evident against her belly. It still wasn't too late to say this was a mistake. The lie hung on her lips unspoken.

She tilted her head back to let the kiss go deeper. Their tongues pushed in and pulled away. They played a familiar game and yet it was completely different. He was a man now and not a teenager. His skilled kiss lacked the rough innocence of youth. She couldn't think about the women who taught him how to kiss better. He should have been learning with her.

His teeth nipped at her lips. He moved to her neck and taunted her with hot wet circles from his tongue. She ran her hands over his back. His solid muscles flexed under her touch. She had been missing him for so long and didn't even know how much until this moment. He had found her when she hadn't realized she'd been lost.

He said something against her neck. His lips moved between the kisses, but she couldn't hear what he said.

She turned his head to look at him. "I didn't hear that. I don't have in my hearing aids."

"You're wearing them now?"

"Well, not now." She hadn't thought to put them in when she left the house. It could take a long time before using them was second nature.

He choked out a laugh. "Sorry. I meant recently. I'm glad you're doing that."

"I'm not so sure I am. But we'll see." Hearing aids weren't the answer she wanted to her problem, and they caused others.

"They don't change you. Don't let anyone tell you they do." He narrowed his eyes as if he tried to read her mind filled with all the negative thoughts floating around in there.

"I'll send those people to you if they bother me." She had always loved the way he protected her. He was strong in a quiet way. He stood in the corner and watched, but if he suspected she needed him, he would appear by her side. Everyone respected him when they were in school and would not cross him because he was tough when he needed to be.

"You had better." He kissed the tip of her nose. "I'll make sure to look right at you when I'm talking tonight. We can keep a light on if you want. You do want to keep going, right?"

He was giving her an out. She could take it and walk away, leaving them most of their dignity. But she wanted nothing more than to be naked with this man, wrapped around him like really good Christmas paper.

"I do want this. But are you okay? I'm not trying to take advantage of a drunk guy." She probably should've thought of that sooner. If the tables were reversed, he could be arrested for assault. She also didn't want him waking up with any regrets.

"I've sobered up a lot, even if it didn't seem like it. I know exactly what I'm doing and what I want. And what I want is you in my bed."

She kissed him in response. She wanted to be in his bed and would show him how much.

He eased out of the embrace and met her gaze. "I said you tasted good. Better than I remembered. That's what I said against your neck."

"Thank you for telling me. I don't want to miss a thing between us."

"Is there an us?"

"Tonight there is."

"And if I want more?"

"One moment at a time. Can you do that for me?" She didn't want him to get too far ahead of tonight. "I want to focus on the here and now. I have no idea what tomorrow will bring."

"I can't lose you again."

"I can't promise you a lifetime. I don't know what my future holds."

"I don't care about your hearing. It doesn't—couldn't —change how I feel about you. If you go completely deaf, I will learn sign language. Hell, I'll start first thing tomorrow. I will do whatever it takes to make you comfortable and happy. I want you in my life."

"Ford, slow down. I appreciate what you're saying, but the bigger picture is I want my career back. I want to play music. I don't want to stay in town." She stepped away from him, needing the space to breathe.

"I've spent my life missing you. I know that makes me sound weak and pathetic, not like a man at all, but you have to know how I feel. I can't let this night go by without you knowing. I won't pretend that what could happen next doesn't mean anything."

His words jumbled in her head. This conversation couldn't be happening. She hadn't expected it to get out of hand with proclamations of lifetime promises.

"What's happening in your house right now means a lot to me. You mean a lot to me. But I need you to know that I'm leaving as soon as I can figure it all out. My life is playing music." She would trade anything for her hearing to be the way it was so she could live out her days doing the only thing that ever made any sense to her.

"And there's no room for more?" He stepped farther away from her.

"I don't know. Maybe. Please understand I can't make any promises. I won't do that. It isn't fair." She would take him with her, if that was possible, but she knew it wasn't.

He flopped into the chair and ran a hand over his head. "No promises."

"Can you live with that?"

"I can take it one day at a time, but I have to know that you want to try."

"I can only take it one day at a time. I can't promise anything past Christmas." Once she found a way to get back on the road and perform, she had no way of knowing what would happen. They could end up spending more time apart than together. What kind of a relationship would that be? He would learn to resent her.

"I need more than that." He stood. "I have to know you're willing to try."

"I can't make a promise I can't keep."

"Then this night is over."

She turned on her heel, grabbed her coat, then plowed into the night air. The cold breeze shocked her hot skin. Anger and humiliation burned her from the inside out. She needed to get away from there as fast as she could. Coming here had been a mistake that would haunt her.

She rummaged in her pockets for the damn keys but couldn't find them. She hated this old car, stopping her from her quick escape and a chance to hold on to her limited dignity. She wouldn't be able to face Ford. Why couldn't he understand she was trying? Just being here was testing her. She had feelings at risk too. She would die if she lost him all over again. That was why she couldn't promise a commitment.

When he had refused to come with her all those years ago, she had cried the whole train ride down to Nashville. She may have been only eighteen, but the feelings of abandonment had been fast and furious. They were supposed to conquer the world together. They were going to take over the music scene and he had let her get on that train alone. Scared and alone.

Something gripped her shoulder, tugging her. She screamed and pulled away. Her arms flailed. She attempted to fight what might be in her way.

"I'm sorry." Ford held up his hands and moved back. His breath came out in short spurts. "I wasn't sure if you'd hear me calling you. Instead of just saying your name, I grabbed you. I didn't mean to scare you."

She wasn't sure if she would have heard him either. The ringing was happening, but she hadn't paid attention because she was upset.

"What do you want?" Tears threatened to come. She took a deep breath to send them away.

"I shouldn't have told you to go. That was stupid, and I'm angry. Angry at myself for pushing you to do something you're not ready to do. I know better than anyone that you won't be forced into agreeing to my terms."

"You won't be happy if I stay." She wanted him to pull her into his arms and tell her he would wait for her until the end of time.

"I'll be miserable if you go. One day at a time. No promises. I'll live with that."

She searched his face for the truth. His eyes were filled with pain. Pain she had put there. That was exactly what she didn't want to happen.

"I don't want you to get hurt." She couldn't live with herself if she caused him any more torment. He deserved to be happy and have all the things he wanted, even the ones he didn't yet know he wanted.

"I'm a big boy. I can take care of myself. You don't have to worry about me."

She did have to worry about herself, though. She would fall to pieces if she gave him the rest of her heart. She had only survived every other relationship because she hadn't risked anything. For a woman who was more than willing to jump into any risk, truly loving a man was out of her league. Lying with Ford tonight would be like asking her to climb her way to the sun.

"I want to kiss you," he said.

"I want you to kiss me too."

He closed the space between them and cupped her face. The heartache in his eyes was replaced with lust. He brought his lips down on her mouth with a force that wasn't there earlier.

Her body lit up as his tongue pushed her lips open. She wrapped her arms around him, pulling him close. Her hands dove under his shirt, unable to resist the need to touch. Her attraction to him was merciless and would punish her when this ended badly. His skin was cool from the night air. He sucked in a breath and eased out of the kiss.

"Let's go inside."

They hurried into the bedroom. Their mouths joined again and the talking ceased. She guided his hand to her breast. He held her close and teased her through the fabric of her sweatshirt. She stepped back and removed her hoodie and the tee underneath. She hadn't bothered to put a bra on when he called.

His eyes widened and that fantastic smile exploded, lighting up his crinkles. "You don't wear a bra anymore?"

"I didn't bother to put it on when you called. I was ready for bed, remember?"

"It's a nice surprise. I think I'll join you." He undid the buttons on his shirt. She stilled his hands.

"Let me." Keeping her gaze on his, she worked each button free. Her fingers trembled over the cotton. His skin was smooth and soft as she undressed him.

With the last button undone, she pushed the shirt off his arms. His chest was coated with only a smattering of hair over his pecs. Her heart picked up speed. She didn't want to wait to wrap her legs around him.

"May I?" He pushed her sweatpants over her hips but stopped before they were too far down.

Always the gentleman who took care of her in ways she didn't know she needed. He gave her the space to make her own decisions, like tonight. He never pushed, and she had never appreciated that until now.

"Yes, please." She helped him the rest of the way with her hands over his. She stepped out of the sweats, leaving nothing but her purple hipster panties. He dragged his gaze over her body to her toes and then back up to her face.

She wasn't one to be uncomfortable around her lover. She worked out because she needed to be in good shape to run around a stage for two hours every night. That made her very accepting of her body. Too bad she couldn't accept her ears, but that was because they failed her. She also liked sex. It was that simple. But standing before Ford, exposed, her stomach twisted in on itself. Being with him was like being a teenager, unsure, awkward. She wanted to be a better lover than he remembered.

"You are beautiful." He traced a finger down the side of her breast, setting her skin ablaze.

"So are you." She placed a hand on the center of his chest. His heart beat under her touch. That was how she heard the music sometimes, by the vibrations against her. His heart made a beautiful tempo all for her.

He tilted his head and narrowed his eyes. "Not hot?"

"That too." She moved closer to work free his belt. He stepped out of his pants and kicked them to the side.

He stood before her void of clothing. He had the kind of body love songs were written about. He was everything and more. Just like she remembered.

They kissed again. They started slow as if there was no urgency or restlessness to what they were doing, but quickly, like dry wood taking flame, their movements became more hurried.

"Dance with me." He locked his fingers through hers.

"Now? Like this?" Was he teasing her because she couldn't hear music the same way? Impossible. Ford wasn't like that. He had known about her problems back when they were kids. He never cared that he had to repeat himself. He didn't even think about it when she moved to sit on his right side so she could hear better with her left ear. He didn't expect her to be anything more than she was even when her hearing made her less.

"Exactly like this."

She didn't know what he had in mind, but she was game. She put her other hand on his shoulder. "There's no music."

"We don't need music." He turned her around, pressing his front into her back.

His arm circled her waist to hold her close. His

mouth was beside her ear. He hummed a tune. The sweet sound filled her up. She pressed against him, and he moaned in response. Their hips swayed.

His free hand massaged her breast. The swaying grew into an erotic dance. She wanted more and reached around to grab his butt.

"No touching, please," he said.

"Why not?" She kept her hand on his backside.

"That's not how the dance goes." He removed her hand, then rested his on her abdomen. His other arm continued to hold her pressed against him.

"You have dance rules?" She could still participate in this little dance and grinded her backside into him.

"I do. You can keep doing that, because it's hot and I like it, but you have to listen to my other rules. I'm a principal. Everyone listens to me." He kissed her neck.

"I'm so glad that wasn't serious." She chuckled and ran her fingers over his arm keeping her against him — exactly where she wanted to be.

"Not a chance, lady." His teeth nipped at her ear. The hand on her abdomen slipped lower until he rested inside her panties.

"A lot of heat in here," he whispered against her ear.

"I heard that."

"I was hoping." He swayed his hips more, taking her hips with him. They picked up speed again, as if the tempo of the imaginary song did too. Her heart matched the pace as they stayed pressed together, his erection hard against her soft bottom.

"Ford, I want to touch you."

"Not yet." His hand moved inside her panties. His finger slid lower and into her heat.

Her knees buckled, but he held her against him with his strong arm. He played her like an instrument he had mastered. He kissed her neck while his hand dipped and returned in a smooth motion. His movements increased, then shifted down into a lower gear, dragging out the pleasure and driving her crazy. He taunted and teased until she could do nothing more than writhe against him while her body dripped with sweat. She was sure her legs would not hold her up another second. But he never let her go over the edge, always knowing how much to give and how much to withhold to make the delicious ecstasy last.

"Ford, please, I need more." Her voice belonged to someone else, someone on the verge of extinction, begging for mercy. She wanted to feel all of him inside her and end the ache that built inside her with every touch from his expert hand.

"I've got you, baby." He continued to hold her against him as he stroked her center, manipulating her as if she were a violin that he could push to perform under his hectic bow playing.

"I can't stand up any longer." All of her muscles wanted to give up and give in to the pulsing.

"Get on your knees on the bed." He released his grip but held her hand as she climbed with shaking legs onto the king-size bed.

"Are you going to let me touch you?" She turned to see him better.

"Not yet." He placed himself behind her again and held her close once more. She rested her head on his chest, helpless to do much else.

"Why not?"

"Because I have fantasized having you in my arms like this many times." He left small kisses along her neck.

"Fantasized when you were in bed with other women?" Her fingers trailed his muscular thigh. He didn't stop her this time.

"Yup." He continued to kiss her neck.

"No wonder your wife left you." Even though it was a joke, secretly she was pleased about being the woman occupying his mind. That knowledge gave her a power she didn't know she had.

"Fantasizing is healthy." His lips worked her shoulder. His hand pushed her panties down to her knees. Between his arm pinning her against him and her underwear around her legs, she didn't have too many places to go.

She didn't want to go anywhere. Her body responded to his touch like no one else's. It was as if no time had gone by at all between them. She wanted to open herself to him completely.

"I think fantasizing might not be such a good thing when you're picturing your old girlfriend." She bent forward and put her hands on the bed, sending her backside right into him. She glanced over her shoulder.

"Jesus." he growled.

The talking ended there. He gripped her hips and pressed his tip against her. Her center vibrated, wanting him all the way. He still didn't give in to her. His hand returned to work her over while she stayed on her hands and knees.

They rocked that way, him behind her, his hand in control, until her heart almost burst out of her ribs. When the anticipation threatened to tear her in two, he thrust inside her. Gripping her waist, he gave her exquisite pleasure. She rose up to her knees again and turned her head to kiss him.

Their mouths locked. She reached behind him to hold his head, needing to touch him. He kept her close, moving in and out, taking her higher and higher until she burst wide open and fell for miles, not sure if she would ever land. Calling his name the whole way.

CHAPTER NINETEEN

Ford woke to a dark room, except for the reading light on his headboard, and Nyx sleeping beside him. She lay sprawled on her stomach. Her dark hair spilled down her creamy back. The sheets gathered at her waist, covering her sexy bottom half.

He pulled the blanket over her. The room was chilly. He hadn't bothered to turn up the heat when they came back from the bar. Nyx had turned his temperature all the way up with that incredible mouth and the way her body moved with his.

His head pounded with reminders of the tequila he drank earlier. That choice to drink until he couldn't think straight put Nyx in his bed. Maybe having one too many wasn't all bad. If he hadn't been too drunk to drive, he would not have called her to come take him home. He would have reasoned away his need to see her. He would have allowed logic and pride to stop what they both wanted to happen. He had no idea she was still attracted to him. All the years apart, and they could have been together. She never said she had missed him or regretted being without him, but she had thrown herself completely into what they shared tonight.

He wanted to make love to her again but wouldn't wake her. The headache might be a problem once they got going anyway. His stomach started to twist and gurgle simply sitting there.

He shoved his legs into his sweats, padded out into the kitchen, then downed more ibuprofen with two glasses of water. He placed the cold glass against his head for some relief.

Where did they go from here? She had been clear about no promises of a future. And he had agreed.

That might have been shortsighted. How was he going to let her go this time? Another chance to be with her wasn't coming around again. And he sure as hell wouldn't watch some other guy weasel in and steal his woman while she figured out what she wanted.

He set the glass down. She wasn't his woman. She wasn't anyone's woman except her own. That didn't mean he wasn't jealous of the idea that a man in her music world would have the power to take her. Tonight sure made a mess of things. Tequila was not his friend. Sober, he would not have become invested and let her go back to her life. Now he was screwed. He was hopelessly in love with her. Kind of pathetic for an almost middle-aged man with a practical career.

He turned on the coffee maker. Morning would arrive soon. The light of day would force them to deal with what they shared. She would either run, which he would bet on, or she would try with him. His head hurt more, trying to make sense of it all.

"Ford?" Nyx came into the kitchen wearing his dress shirt.

The material came to her knees. Most of the buttons were still undone, revealing a hint of cleavage. His groin pulsed at the sight of her. He was a goner where this woman was concerned. He had no chance of survival.

"Hey. Did I wake you?" He went to her and pulled her into his arms. He needed her soft curves against him.

"I thought I heard a door closing. Then I thought I must be dreaming because I'm not sure how well I can hear a door closing, but I rolled over and you were gone." She pushed a strand of his hair off his forehead. Her touch tingled over his skin.

"Sorry if I woke you. My head is pounding. I needed to get up and get some caffeine in me."

"Too much tequila." She smirked.

"Guilty as charged."

"Do you want me to rub your neck?"

"I'll be fine after a cup of coffee. Do you want some?" He eased out of the embrace to grab mugs and the milk, and to give himself a chance to play it cool. He had come on strong and needed to rein himself in.

"No, thanks. If you don't mind, I thought I'd take a quick shower and then head home." She hitched a thumb over her shoulder.

"Sure. Help yourself. Clean towels are in the closet in the bathroom." He turned away to keep from showing any kind of disappointment. He had worn his heart on his sleeve enough tonight. He bit back the words about where they go from here. Will he see her again? How long did he have to wait? And a hundred other questions banging around in his head, demanding to get out. Playing it cool was harder than he realized.

"Did you want to join me?"

He turned to find the shirt on the floor and Nyx standing there naked and bold and beautiful. His breath caught in his throat.

"Hell yes, I do." He closed the space between them and picked her up. She wrapped her legs around him, threw back her head, and laughed. A light filled her ice-blue eyes that wasn't there before.

This was the Nicole he remembered when they were young and the one he saw on stage when she performed. She was wild and free and there was no taming her. He had been smart enough to let her be her until she wanted to leave him. Then he had wanted her to change into someone she could never become. He might be doing that again, but he wouldn't think about that while she had her naked body wrapped around him. Instead, he would enjoy what she was offering. It might not last.

He took her into the bathroom, turned on the shower, and waited for the water to warm. Then he pressed her against the tiled wall while the hot water poured over their bodies. He made love to her until she cried out his name, their gazes locked the whole time. He gave in to release when he was certain she was done. They stood in the shower, holding each other, their chests heaved from the exertion. Making love to her was going to kill him. And there was nothing he could do to stop it.

"Do you want a minute to yourself to clean up?" He would step out until she was done before using the shower himself for its intended purpose. He had to pick up Delaney from his parents' house early this morning and get back to real life.

Nyx grabbed the bar of soap. "Turn around. I'll scrub your back."

He faced the wall and put his hands against it. Water beat on his shoulders and neck. His headache receded into the background with Nyx's hands all over him. The smell of cucumber and melon filled the small space.

He turned and cupped her face. She gave him a devilish smile.

"Kiss me, Mr. McKay."

"I thought you needed to get home." He didn't think he could be ready for her between the headache and all their earlier activity, but this woman's touch turned him on like no one else. He wanted her hands everywhere over and over.

"I do. But there's this hot guy in the shower with me. Hard to pass up an opportunity." She wrapped her soapy hand around him.

Real life could wait another ten minutes. He pressed his lips to hers.

Someone banged on the bathroom door. He jumped out of her hold. Nyx backed up and hit the shower wall.

"Did you hear that?" He moved her behind him.

"No. What was it?" She pressed against him.

"Someone's at the door."

"The bathroom door?" Nyx looked around as if trying to find someplace to hide.

"Stay here." He stepped out, then wrapped a towel around his waist. Still dripping, he slipped out of the bathroom.

He didn't think they were being robbed. Robbers

didn't knock and the crime rate was low in Candlewood Falls. But he had heard that knock. He was sure of it.

Dawn had crested sometime while they were busy loving and touching. The light outside the windows painted the day in shades of gray and threw the bedroom into shadows. No one was there. He went out into the hall. Voices drifted toward him. He hung his head and listened for a minute before returning to Nyx.

She had come out of the shower and hurried to pull on her clothes. "Did you call the police?"

"It's my mother and Delaney."

"Who knocked on the door? Please tell me it wasn't Delaney. I have to get out of here. I'll climb out the window." She turned away.

He grabbed her wrist. "You don't have to sneak out of here. We're not kids anymore. We're two consenting adults."

"But your daughter is going to see me come out of your bedroom at the ass crack of dawn. What about the example you need to set?"

"I'll get dressed and go out. You wait five minutes before following. My mother is going to know and never let us hear the end of it, but Delaney won't put it together. She'll think you were just in the bathroom. She's too young to get the details. And if she asks about it, I'll say you slept on the couch. Okay?"

"If you say so."

"I do." He threw on clean clothes.

Nyx's eyes grew wide. "Your shirt is still on the kitchen floor."

"I'll deal with it." He kissed her, then closed the door behind him. He could have done without the encounter and wondered why his mother had returned Delaney early.

"Good morning," he said, entering the kitchen as if this were any other day.

"Hi, Daddy. I knocked on your door, but you were in the shower." Delaney smiled at him with a milk mustache and a Christmas bow on her head.

His plan to make it look as if he and Nyx were not in the shower might not work after all. He had hoped his mother had been the one at the door. "Did you need something?"

"I want to get a Christmas tree today."

"Is that why you came home early?" He looked to his mother and held her gaze.

"Delaney is very excited about the tree. She can't sleep." Golda looked put together with her long sweater and matching silk scarf around her head. His mother was a classic and a hippie simultaneously.

"Santa needs a place to put the presents. We can't wait to get a tree. He'll know we didn't care enough to make it nice for him." Delaney wiped her mouth with the back of her hand.

Golda handed over a napkin and shook her head.

"How will he know that we didn't care?"

"Daddy, Santa knows everything. You said that yourself." Delaney rolled her eyes with perfection.

Nothing like having his words thrown at him. "Yes, of course. How could I forget. We'll get a tree today."

Delaney jumped up and down, clapping her hand. Her bow slipped from her head.

"Did you wake up Lolli and Pop so you could come

home? That wasn't very nice. You don't like being woken up."

"I couldn't sleep either. I was already in the kitchen with a cup of tea when Delaney joined me. We decided to take a ride and make breakfast for you. Oh, by the way, I put your shirt in the laundry, dear." Golda lifted her brows right under that scarf.

Heat burned his cheeks. Even if he was an adult, he still couldn't admit to his mother he had sex. Just like he never dared to think of his parents like that. Golda had to know what he'd been up to. Nyx's car was in the driveway and his wasn't. Leaving a shirt on the floor wasn't something he made a habit of doing. At least Delaney hadn't seen Nyx when she came into the bedroom to knock on the door.

"Thank you." He checked the time over the stove. Nyx hadn't joined them. He sincerely hoped she hadn't climbed out the window to save face.

"It looks as if you started to make coffee but were sidetracked." His mother pointed to the coffee maker. The coffee, mugs, and milk were still on the counter. Her lips quivered in a smile.

"I can make more." He was never going to hear the end of this. His mother was enjoying the torture.

"No, let me. I think you left something behind you might want to check on before it gets lost."

Delaney narrowed her eyes and looked between Golda and him. "Did you lose something, Daddy? I could help you find it."

"That's okay, sweetie. I didn't lose anything. Lolli doesn't know what she's saying. She's getting old. I'll be right back." He hurried from the kitchen before his mother said anything more.

He would grab Nyx by the hand and they would just face the consequences. He would insist Nyx slept on the couch and when Delaney realized she hadn't seen Nyx either when she came into his room, he'd distract her with sweets. He didn't believe in bribery, but this was an emergency.

He took a deep breath before opening his bedroom door. Things could have been worse. Delaney could have caught them in the middle of sex. This was an easy fix. He turned the knob and was met with a blast of cold air. The curtain billowed in the breeze.

That stubborn woman had climbed out the window after all.

CHAPTER TWENTY

Nyx couldn't believe she had taken off like a coward, but she couldn't face Delaney. Whoever had knocked on the bathroom door had come into the bedroom and would have noticed her absence. How could she walk into the kitchen as if it was the most normal thing and look that child in the eye? It would be hard enough to hold Golda's gaze and she had known Nyx was sleeping with her son at seventeen. She had almost caught them once back then too. She was sure Golda had only stayed on the other side of her young son's door because she knew Nyx was in Ford's bed. History had a funny way of repeating itself.

This way would be much better. She could retain some of her dignity, even if it was fabricated, and she could spare Ford having to tell his little girl that a woman was in the shower with him—that woman being her singing teacher.

She walked around the front of the house and rang the bell.

The door opened and Ford glared at her. "Where did you go?" he said under his breath. She almost didn't catch it all.

"I climbed out the window. It was too embarrassing to... you know." She tried to indicate with her head what she was talking about. She didn't want to say too much in case little ears were nearby.

"Your hair is still wet."

"I did the best I could without turning on the hair dryer." She had towel dried her hair with a fury, but her long, thick locks wouldn't dry. The towel caused her hair to stick up in too many directions as if she had been electrocuted. She had pulled it back and tried to secure it with a pencil, but several pieces fell out of the twist and around her face.

"I said I'd take care of it. You didn't have to sneak away like we have anything to be ashamed of."

"This way is better. You can pretend I popped over."

"They saw your car."

She hadn't thought about that.

The door swung open farther. Ford flinched. Golda smiled at her in that elegant but casual way only she could pull off.

"Hello, Nicole. How nice of you to stop by this morning." Golda gave her the once-over. She also didn't have her coat and it was freezing with her wet hair.

"Hello, Golda. You're looking lovely. That scarf is beautiful."

Golda touched the back of her head. "Why, thank you. Please join us for breakfast. You look like you might be hungry—and cold."

"I will." She stepped past Ford.

Golda leaned over and said into her ear, "Are you coming over to pick up your car or your coat or both?"

Her mouth stopped working, caught in the lie even though she suspected Golda knew. She would always be that girl dating Ford instead of a grown woman.

"A mother always knows. No point in denying it. I'm happy for you both." Golda sashayed into the kitchen.

"You should've come out with me and saved us both the embarrassment." Ford shook his head.

"Sorry. I thought I was helping."

"Let's get this over with." Ford took her hand, but she pulled it away.

He stopped and looked right at her. "What gives?"

She wasn't ready to announce anything despite Golda figuring it out. She and Ford had spent one night together. The best night she'd experienced in ages other than being on stage. She hoped to have more with him, but she meant it when she had said she needed to take it slow.

Her entire life was often on public view. Very few things were just for her. She wanted this time with Ford to be for them only. If things progressed and they were going to stay together after she left town, then maybe she would announce it to the world. When that happened, the cameras would flash and the questions would demand answers. She had no interest in entertaining that now and she was rather certain her practical, logical man would feel the same way once the limelight blinded them.

"Nicole, did you hear me?"

"I heard you." She didn't have to hear him. The hurt twisted his features and broke her heart. She was no good for him. She couldn't give him what he wanted. How could she? He expected something too big.

"Then what's going on?"

"Your mother already knows. Let's leave it at that, okay? We don't need to do more." She hurried into the kitchen before Ford could say anything else.

"Hi, Delaney." She high-fived the adorable girl. "I love that bow. Is it a new one?"

"I made it last night at Lolli's. What are you doing here?" Delaney had Ford's smile. When she looked up at Nyx with a curiosity and little crinkles around her happy eyes, it hurt to breathe.

"I stopped by to see you." She brushed Delaney's hair away from her shoulder. Being around her warmed Nyx in a way she had never experienced before. No other child had stolen her heart like this.

"Good thing we came back in time, Lolli. If we had waited, we would have missed Nyx."

"Good thing," Golda said. "I'll get breakfast started."

"Nyx, we're going to buy a Christmas tree today. Do you want to come with us?" Delaney looked at her with expectant eyes.

"Nyx has plans today," Ford said.

"Please?" Delaney held her hands in prayer under her chin. "We won't be gone too long. I know the exact kind of tree I want."

"Oh, gee, I don't want to interfere with a family tradition."

Being out in public could mean someone would see them and take pictures. Ford would be upset by the intrusion into his and his daughter's private life. Or she could admit to herself, she was afraid to start a relationship.

She still hadn't addressed most of the issues regarding her hearing with the press. Her assistant, Mindy, had fended off some of the inquiries, but not all. Someone could snap a picture or ask for a selfie with her or worse, want to know when she'd be back. She didn't want to be faced with talking to anyone if her tinnitus was in overdrive. She could wear her hearing aids... was that going to be her only answer? She didn't want it to be even if the doctors said that was it.

"Traditions are meant to be changed." Golda pulled a carton of eggs out of the fridge.

"Mom," Ford said with a warning.

"I'm just saying." Golda returned to her task of whisking up breakfast.

"I don't have to come," she said to Ford. "I understand. This is your family time."

"If you don't mind being seen with the high school principal, you're welcome to join us." His words dripped with sarcasm and the hurt in his eyes was evident.

She deserved that after sneaking out the window and refusing to hold his hand moments ago. Not her finest hour, but lately none of them were. Running had always been her immediate reaction when times became too difficult to deal with.

"I don't care that you're a high school principal." She cared about hurting him by starting something she couldn't finish. If her hearing came back tomorrow, she would go back to her life. What kind of life would she be able to give him, here in Candlewood Falls? She would have to reinvent herself.

"You don't want to give people something to talk about by being seen with me. Someone might misunderstand."

"Delaney," Golda said, looking between Nyx and Ford. "Can you help me a minute? I want to grab some mint from Daddy's plant out back."

"Now?" Delaney whined.

"Yes, please." Golda waved her over.

"It's cold out." Delaney's bottom lip stuck out.

"Grab your coat." Golda grabbed her own.

Delaney hopped off the stool and the two slipped out the door.

"Your mother is trying to give us privacy because you're getting angry."

"Too bad she hadn't thought about that before she came over." He ran a hand over his hair.

"She didn't know I was here."

"And you didn't want her to know, either. And you're right, I am upset. You ran out on me this morning. After everything we shared last night, you took off." His top lip curled up and his nostrils flared with each word.

"I didn't completely run out. I came to the door. I was trying to spare us some embarrassment. I wasn't leaving this time." He would always hold her decision to go without him to Nashville against her. He would never get past that time.

"But eventually you will," he said as if he read her mind.

"I told you I couldn't promise anything. Why won't you understand that?" Anger bubbled in her belly.

He turned his back and walked away. She wanted to reach out and turn him around because she didn't want to miss what he said, but she stayed rooted to the ground. She wouldn't run away from him and she wasn't going to run after him right now either. He was acting like a jerk.

He leaned on the counter with his hands and hung his head. She forced her legs to stay still. She wanted to ease his pain because she had caused so much of it for him, but her life was at stake.

He finally turned to her. "I don't want to be a fling that kept you busy while you were in town. I need more."

"What happened to one day at a time?"

"I can't, Nicole. I'm sorry. I want to act like I don't care, but I do. You'll have to decide."

"Please be patient with me. I'm trying. I didn't get in my car and drive away. I'm standing right here asking you not to be mad at me and not to send me away." She bit back words of love that begged to be set free. Her heart ached with the love for this man and now his daughter. It would be easy to tell him what he wanted to hear, but she couldn't give up on fixing her hearing and her career just yet. She also couldn't bear the idea of hurting them both, because she would.

"You were happy this morning. It's the first time I saw that kind of happiness in your eyes since you've been back. I'd like to think I had something to do with that." He crossed his arms over his chest.

He did, more than he knew. When she was with him, she could be herself without the worry of being a weaker version. He accepted her, flaws and all. "It's easy to be with you."

"That sounds to me like something you'd say to

someone you want to spend time with." He closed the space between them.

She wanted to drown in his nearness. Everything was right in her world with Ford close to her side. She could curl against his strong chest and know that he would take care of her. If only she could let go and fall into what he was asking for.

"I do want to spend time with you. I don't know what the future holds, though."

"No one does." He placed a kiss on her lips and she didn't stop him.

She moaned when he pushed his tongue into her mouth. The powers that be needed to help her because she was quickly losing control where Ford was concerned.

Golda and Delaney came through the door, banging it against the wall. "Oops. That slipped out of my hand," Golda said with a shrug and a laugh.

At least, they moved apart before Delaney caught them. She carried a bundle of the mint, bringing with her its sweet scent, and blocked most of her view.

"Nyx, did you decide to come with Daddy and me?" Delaney put the mint on the counter, then looked up at her with expectant eyes.

Ford arched a brow but didn't say anything. He would leave her to make the decision and live or die by it. She knew what he wanted, but did she want that too?

She glanced between the two adults and Delaney. Now or never. "Yes, I would like that very much. Thank you for inviting me."

Delaney threw herself into Nyx and hugged her around the waist. "We're going to have so much fun. I need to make you a bow." And the little girl ran off like the wind.

Golda laughed. "She likes you."

"I like her too." A lot. "I'd better get home. I need to change. What time should I meet you at the tree lot?"

"I'll pick you up," Ford said.

"That's okay. I can meet you. Then you don't have to go out of your way." If she had her own car, she could make a quick exit if it became necessary.

"Nicole, dear, let the man act like a gentleman and pick you up. You allowed him to stick his tongue down your throat in the kitchen. A ride is hardly a commitment."

CHAPTER TWENTY-ONE

The air smelled of pine and possibilities. Nyx smiled to herself as she weaved between spruces, cypresses, and Douglas firs. She, Ford, and Delaney had searched for a tree over the past thirty minutes. Her tinnitus had receded in part due to her hearing aids. She had decided to give them another try this afternoon. She kept her hair down to cover them from spying eyes.

The other part was the enjoyment of being outside in a tiny forest with people she liked and trying to make a little girl happy by finding the perfect Christmas tree and wearing the bow Delaney had made for her, a blue bow with yellow flowers. This outing was the most stress-free time she had experienced since arriving in Candlewood Falls. Well, except for making love to Ford. But that was different.

Gray clouds hung low in the sky as if stretching on tiptoes would be enough for her to run her fingers into their cold, soft bellies. Damp air settled against her skin. Winter hadn't received the notice that she had arrived too soon. Autumn still had some time left but had given up her hold as if she knew she couldn't win over the more determined winter.

Nyx was in the autumn of her life. Was she holding on too tightly to things better left in the past? Could she let go and move forward?

The tree farm was filled with people doing much of the same thing they were. Families stopped at intervals to admire or reject a tree. Many took photos of their escapade, laughing the whole time. Nyx tried to shrink inside her coat. So far, no one had noticed who she was. The large sunglasses and the scarf that came up to her chin may help or no one cared out here about meeting a famous person. They had more important things to do. Or just maybe, she was already forgotten from people's fickle memories.

Ford turned to her and smiled. Her heart wanted to reach across the space between them. When she looked at him, his tall, thin frame, his broad shoulders, long legs, confident smile, and loving eyes, she could almost surrender to what he wanted from her. Time with him made sense. Her life away from him made sense too— two railroad tracks that did not cross.

"This one." Delaney jumped up and down in front of a ten-foot Douglas fir.

Ford choked out a laugh. "That one's a little big, kiddo."

"It's smaller than the one at Lolli and Pop's."

"True, but they have a bigger house. How about this one over here? It's the same kind but a lot shorter." Ford pointed out another fir nearby.

"Nyx, do you like it?" Delaney tapped her finger against her chin, studying the tree and her.

"I think it could use a few of your bows. Maybe a few small red ones on some of the branches? Then it would be perfect." She fingered a branch and hopefully twisted her face into an inquisitive expression to match Delaney's.

"I agree." Delaney punched the air above her head.

"We have a winner," Ford said.

"Can we get hot cocoa now?" Delaney said.

"Right after I pay for the tree." Ford signaled for the teenager who carried the trees up to the front. "I'll be right back. Stay here."

Ford hurried off.

"Will you help us decorate it?" Delaney adjusted her red and black bow.

"If that's what you and your dad want." She wanted it too. She hadn't decorated a tree in ages because there had never been any point. No one had been special enough to share the moment with.

"We'll have so much fun. We have lots of ornaments. Dad keeps them in the attic. We fill the whole tree, and we play Christmas music, and we sing. Dad is a better singer than I am."

"You're getting there. You've improved a lot, and you love it. That's all that matters."

"Should I sing a Christmas song at the showcase instead of the one I've been practicing? My favorite is 'Jingle Bells.' What's yours?" Delaney slid her hand into hers. The small gesture startled her, but she wrapped her fingers around Delaney's.

"'Have Yourself A Merry Little Christmas'. Judy

Garland's version. Do you know who she is?" They walked a little toward the front. She didn't want to go too far. Ford would be back soon, but there was a young couple watching them from a distance. Nyx wanted a little protection behind a bigger tree.

"I don't know who that is." Delaney scrunched up her adorable face.

"She's Dorothy in the *Wizard of Oz*."

"Oh. She's wonderful." Delaney's eyes flew open with realization.

"I know. I feel that way about her too."

"Will you sing it for me now?"

"I'm out of practice." She didn't want to butcher one of the most beautiful holiday songs ever. Her hearing was adequate at the moment, but she could risk making a fool of herself by trying to tackle that song, and if that couple heard... She didn't want to think about it.

"We can practice together at my next lesson."

Everything was solvable to a nine-year-old. She admired that quality. "Sure thing."

Ford bounded toward them, rubbing his hands together. "We're all set. Ready for some hot cocoa?"

"Yes." Delaney ran off toward the stand.

"Stay close," Ford called after her. "She's a bundle of energy all the time."

"I see that. She's cute."

"I'm very lucky." He stood facing her, blocking out the rest of the world.

If she held his gaze, everything around them dropped away. The couple watching her moments ago mattered no longer. Her thoughts drifted to wanting to touch him.

She didn't have to pretend to enjoy this moment, but it still scared her.

"Tell me what happened at the bar last night. You never said." She needed the conversation to continue to keep her hands from roaming over his torso.

He laced his fingers through hers. "Is this okay?"

"The hand-holding? Very much." She squeezed his hand. They started to walk toward the hot cocoa stand. He knew what she needed, and she didn't know how he could be so in tune with her. He truly was like a well-rehearsed love ballad.

"I did something stupid last night before I texted you."

"Besides the drinking?" She pushed into him to be playful.

"Very funny. After a few too many tequilas, I decided to go on stage and play with the band."

"That's fantastic. Good for you." She tried to control her enthusiasm, but she failed. He had always been a solid musician who could've made things happen if he had tried. Together they would've been fantastic, like Johnny and June or Garth and Trisha.

"It was a disaster." He told her what had happened and how hopeless he had felt.

"Oh, Ford. I'm sorry. It was the tequila, not you." She stopped walking and placed a hand on his chest. His heart beat beneath her touch like thunder. She could write a melody from his heartbeat.

"It's me. Trust me. I had no business getting up there. I just wanted to prove you wrong."

"You still can."

"Don't dare me, Nicole. We aren't kids anymore,

climbing over rocks that crossed the stream." He narrowed his eyes.

"You could take the dare, you know. Just once."

"Not this one. My playing days are over. I'm going to stay in my lane where I belong."

"Would you come on stage with me?" She had asked him that question before and blew up her life. She had cried for weeks when he had stayed behind.

"I don't think so. Let me watch you from the side. I'm better there. You said so yourself."

"I should not have said you were watching your life go by. That was uncalled for. You have a lovely life with your parents who love and support you; your mom is great, and you have Delaney and a community that respects you. You're going to become the superintendent. That's an accomplishment. Anyone can do what I do."

He grabbed her hand and kissed her fingers. "That is not true. No one can do what you do. You're special. I'm trying to make a difference in a quieter way. It's worth it most days."

Maybe it was the closeness of the overcast sky and its soft, brisk breeze, or it was the way Ford's gaze searched her face with a hunger, but she wanted him by her side for as long as he would stand there.

"You are an honorable man who cares about other people—even me. Never sell yourself short." She cupped the back of his neck and pulled him to her.

He slid his hands inside her coat and pressed her against his hard body. She moaned as his tongue swept her mouth. He bent her back to take the kiss deeper. Her hair fell away from her face. She didn't care about any of the other patrons watching them. She wanted the kiss to go on and on.

Applause and jeers broke them apart. He jumped back, and she lost her balance, falling on her butt. Laughter erupted. A group of patrons held out their phones in her direction.

"Hey, Nyx, are you sleeping with him?"

"When are you going to tour again?"

"Are you deaf?"

She scrambled to her feet. Ford held out a hand, but she brushed him away. "That's enough, guys. Let's put your phones away and give us some privacy please."

She should keep her mouth shut. That was the best way to handle the situation. All those phones were probably recording everything she did. But she wanted to tell them to go away, to leave them alone. Ford would hate the attention.

She turned, and he was gone. He had hurried to the hot cocoa stand and scooped up Delaney. They rushed toward the parking lot.

"Did your boyfriend leave you?"

"Isn't that the high school principal?"

"Can I have your autograph?"

"Leave us alone." She sneered and fisted her hands.

"She's mad." More laughing.

She was helpless to stop them or save Ford. She was helpless to do anything except run. But if she ran, they would chase her like prey. She had to pull herself together or her meltdown would go viral, if it hadn't already.

Because she was and always would be impulsive

Nicole Wilde, she flipped the bird as an attempt to have the last word and slipped between the trees.

CHAPTER TWENTY-TWO

"Mr. McKay?" Beth stood in the doorway to Ford's office. Her lips were pressed into a thin line. Her gaze darted around the room, but she wouldn't look at him.

The whole school day had been a plethora of extinguishing one fire after another. It was almost three o'clock and he was ready to get out of there and see Nyx.

"Yes?"

"Mr. Turner from the board of education is here. He'd like to speak with you."

"Now?"

"Yes. Should I send him in?" Beth's cheeks bloomed red.

"What's going on?"

"I don't know."

He was pretty sure she was lying. "Send him in." He moved some files off his visitor's chair.

He had avoided Nyx all week after the video went

viral of them kissing and her giving those people the middle finger. He had arrived at his parents' house after Delaney's singing lesson had ended and she was gone. His mother had tried to give him a piece of her mind, but he had dodged her too. He also hadn't answered Nyx's texts with more than one-word answers and excuses of being busy with work.

Nyx didn't deserve his cold shoulder. He was acting like a coward. The publicity wasn't her fault. He had wanted her to kiss him in the worst way in that Christmas tree lot, but he had a child to raise and a school to manage. Having the principal splashed all over the internet in a public display of affection was a bad look. He needed to apologize for his childish behavior and promise to do better, if she even still wanted him. She had warned him this kind of thing could happen and that he wouldn't like it. She had been right. He wasn't sure he could live his life in the public eye that way. He didn't want that for Delaney. He might have to let Nyx go, after all. The thought crushed him. All he had ever wanted was another chance with her.

"Good afternoon, Mr. McKay." Mr. Turner, with his bald head, advanced into the office. He was the same height as Ford, but he had more of a brick house build. The man probably had played football in his day if his thick neck was any indication. He wore an expensive-looking black wool coat with a black suit underneath. His tie was power red and his shoes polished to a shine. Mr. Turner wanted to be noticed, if Ford had to guess.

"Hello, Mr. Turner. What brings you by today?" He didn't ask the man to sit.

This wasn't a social call. Mr. Turner had never been

here before, but he was married to Megan Turner. The parent who had come into the office only a few weeks ago, claiming her son Jake didn't deserve a seventy-five on his English paper. She must've sent her husband in to get the grade changed. Parents often believed when the father showed up, situations would be taken seriously by the teachers and staff. Fathers weren't usually the front line when it came to school matters. They were the stealth reinforcements. Well, not for him.

"I have a matter to discuss with you." Turner stood with his feet apart and hands clasped in front of him.

"Is this about Jake?" Might as well cut to the chase and end the power play Turner seemed to be looking for. This was his school. He called the shots around here.

"I already took care of the paper, no thanks to you. The teacher came around to seeing things my way. I'm here about a school situation and one that needs to be addressed immediately. I wanted to tell you myself so there wasn't any confusion."

Mrs. Lewis had given in? He would need her side of the story, but that little piece of information shook him. Jake deserved that grade.

Ford hadn't heard about any school situation this week either, at least nothing out of the ordinary that would warrant a visit from a board member. More fires to put out, and he was hitting his patience limit.

"Does the superintendent know?" He reported to the super, Gus Elliot, who reported to the board. If a problem arose that required the board's input, Gus would've been at his door by now. Gus was retiring in June, but he still had Ford's back.

"The board didn't feel it was necessary to involve

Gus. We're pulling your application for the superintendent's position." Mr. Turner's eyes were void of emotion as if Ford looked into an empty space.

"Excuse me?" A ringing noise filled his head, jumbling his thoughts. He shook his head. The noise stopped. Was that what Nyx heard all the time? She held it together well, if she did. That constant loud pitch would drive him mad.

"We've decided to pursue other more suitable candidates. We're telling you this now so you can make other arrangements."

"What do you mean other arrangements?"

"If you'd like to pursue a superintendent's position in another school district, we'd understand."

"Are you trying to push me out?" He didn't understand, that was for sure.

"Not at all. You've done a good job as principal."

"The interview process isn't over yet. How do you know I'm not the best candidate for the job? And frankly, I believe I am the best." He had run this school for the past four years without incident. The test scores were up. The sports teams were successful. They offered programs other schools in the county did not and coveted. The school had earned a Blue Ribbon of Excellence award under him, a high honor.

"We're aware of your romantic relationship with the singer. You and she behaved inappropriately for an administrator of this school district. You violated our school conduct policy. You're setting a bad example."

Singer. As if he didn't know Nyx's name. "The singer has a name, and it was just a kiss. People do that in public all the time. I didn't violate anything." A hot flush crawled out of his belly and over his body. His skin broke out in a sweat. The conduct policy didn't say anything about no kissing in public.

"Not that kind of kiss."

"We were not inappropriate. That's ridiculous."

"The board sees it differently. We have to think of the school's reputation and the example you set for the students. You can't go around behaving like you have no control of yourself. These teenagers are impressionable. They will believe they can do what they saw you do."

"Mr. Turner, do you remember being a teenager? Many of those kids are doing way more than kissing by the time they get to this school. Seeing me kiss the woman I care for is hardly in poor taste." He could tell this man how he found Jake feeling up a young lady in the girls' locker room.

"It isn't just the kissing. Your friend was inciting hate. We don't need a riot at the school."

"A riot? Are you for real? This must be some kind of a joke. Nyx wasn't trying to start a fight." He threw his hands up and Turner backed away as if he might get hit.

He needed to stay calm. His livelihood was on the line. If he couldn't be the superintendent, he would be at a dead end as the principal. He would have to stay in this position for another fifteen to twenty years or he'd have to change school districts and possibly move again. He couldn't move away while Delaney was so young.

"There's no joke here. That video clearly showed your girlfriend flirting with a hate crime. The young man who held the phone was a person of color. He was afraid."

He swallowed all the words fighting to get free. Nyx

had done no such thing. That young man was making it all up.

He should've stayed and helped her, but she had pushed him away and he had wanted to get Delaney back to the car before the crowd followed him. He should not have allowed Nyx to handle the whole thing herself. Shit, he had kissed her. He had started the whole thing.

"I wanted to give you the courtesy of telling you in person since you are the school principal."

"No, you came here to tell me this because I wouldn't change your son's grade and you got pissed off. This is your revenge."

"Now who's being ridiculous? I don't need to seek revenge for anything. Jake's grade was changed before this fiasco. Your behavior and the people you choose to associate with are the reason why you are no longer in the running. Your priorities won't be to the school district if you're tangled up with a questionable celebrity. She could be into drugs for all we know. We can't have our principal involved with a drug addict."

"You need to stop disparaging Nyx. I won't allow you to sully her reputation with your lies. Am I clear?" His jaw hurt from clenching it. This man would not come into his office and say hurtful things about Nyx.

"Are you threatening me, Mr. McKay?" Turner pulled his phone out of his coat pocket. "Do I need to call the police?"

"You're nuts. You know that? If I threaten you, you'll know it." He had spent his life not starting any fights, but if someone tried to hurt him or someone he loved, then all bets were off. "I'll fight the board's decision. You can't deny me the interview because of one stupid photo."

"Two videos that show your character. There's nothing to fight. The decision has been made. Good day, Mr. McKay." Turner spun on his heel and marched out of the office.

Ford tried to control his breathing but couldn't suck in enough air, as if he had no control over his lungs. His heart pounded in his throat. His vision blurred.

He moved by a force other than himself and shoved everything off his desk in one swoop. Papers flew. His laptop bounced on the floor, and the screen cracked. His mug tipped over and spilled the dredges from this morning's coffee onto the floor. His lamp shattered. His pens scattered.

"Mr. McKay, are you okay? Do you need help?" Beth said in a voice he could barely hear.

"I'm fine." He was anything but fine. He couldn't tell her, although the mess he made said it all.

"Are you sure?" She hovered like a moth.

"Go away, Beth. For both our sakes," he said through gritted teeth.

She scurried away. He would have to apologize to her, but later. Much later.

He needed to get out of there and grabbed his coat. He hurried to his car. Everything he had worked for, planned for, told himself he believed in, was gone. His future had disappeared like fog under the sun's heat.

His phone rang. Tenna's name appeared on his screen. She was the very last person he wanted to talk to at this moment, but he swiped the screen in case she had something important to say about Delaney.

"What's up, Tenna?"

"Ford? I saw that video of you and that slut singer. I don't want my daughter spending time with that woman." Her voice grated on his last nerve.

"Shut up, Tenna."

She gasped. "What did you say?"

"You heard me. Stop talking. All you do is talk, talk, talk, and never say anything worthwhile. Delaney doesn't need you. Stop pretending like you care because Nyx is back."

"So you are with her."

"I'm hanging up now." He didn't know if he was with Nyx or not and he wasn't about to discuss any of it with his ex-wife. Tenna never cared about their family and she had stopped caring about him a long time ago. He had stuck it out longer than he should have because of his daughter.

"I want Delaney for Christmas."

"You can't have her. She has the showcase Christmas Eve." And even if she didn't, he'd be damned before he'd allow Tenna to have the glory of Christmas morning. She could have time with Delaney later in the day.

"You can't stop me from seeing my child."

"Yes, actually I can. When you gave me full custody without a fight. All the decisions concerning her welfare are mine to make and mine alone. Or did you forget?"

"Then I'll come to the show and take her after."

"Over my dead body." He ended the call before he said or did anything worse.

He started the car and pulled out of the lot, heading to the one person who would make him feel better. Unless she hated him now.

Which she would have every right to.

He hated himself pretty good at the moment.

CHAPTER TWENTY-THREE

Nyx regretted her decision to flip off those people at the Christmas tree farm. She knew better, but she had been embarrassed. Anger had flooded her system and she wanted an ounce of control back because since she returned to Candlewood Falls, control was the last thing she had. Her hearing wasn't something she could fix with the snap of a finger and that was all she wanted.

She couldn't stay in the house any longer and took a walk to the park near her house where she and sisters would go when they were kids. Her mom would take them and watch as they scrambled over the jungle gym or flew high on the swings.

Her feet remembered the way, pulling her along the cracked sidewalk. The park had seen better days with its peeling paint, grass worn down to the hard dirt, and broken seesaws longing for riders. The sun tipped below the barren trees. Daylight would extinguish soon and she would be sitting along in the cold, damp dark. She didn't have anything to warm her insides the way she had at the Christmas tree farm. Ford had ignored her all week.

She sat on the faded and chipping old wooden bench. Ford had every right to be mad. He had Delaney to think about. She wished he would let her apologize at least. After the showcase in a few days, he would never have to see her again. She would stay on her side of town for as long as she remained in Candlewood Falls.

She had an appointment with another specialist in New York City after the New Year. Hopefully, he would tell her something different or point her in a direction she didn't know about. If that happened, she would go back to Nashville and recharge her career. Somehow.

Her phone vibrated in her pocket. She pulled it out and had to read the screen twice to make sure her eyes still worked. Ford was calling.

She put the phone to her ear since she didn't have in her hearing aids. "Ford?"

"Hey. Where are you? I need to talk. If that's okay. I don't mean to steamroll you."

"I'm at the park by my house."

"I'll be there in five. Thank you for seeing me."

"Can I say one thing?"

"Wait till I get there." He ended the call.

The sun dipped further and she snuggled inside her coat. It would become too cold to sit on the bench much longer. She stood and banged her feet on the ground to chase some of the chill away. Ford turned into the small parking lot and beeped his horn. Any sound that she could name without hesitation gave her hope.

He hopped out of the car and waved. "It's warm in the car."

She wasn't sure she wanted to sit so close to him, but she no longer wished to be outside at the sad park that the town had forgotten. She walked over and slid in beside him.

The lines around his mouth turned down. The crease between his brow deepened. His warm eyes were hooded. He turned on the interior lights that offered enough glow for her to read his lips.

"What happened?" she asked.

He turned to face her. "I had to see you. I'm sorry I haven't reached out all week. I've been a jerk."

"It's my fault. I can't control my temper."

"I shouldn't have kissed you in public. I wasn't thinking."

"I like all that no thinking you were doing, but my lifestyle isn't fair to you and Delaney. I should've thought that through and declined your invitation. I will from now on. You won't have to deal with me much longer."

"Don't walk away because of how I responded this week. I need you." He took her hand in his cold one.

"What happened today?"

"The board pulled my application. I'm out of the running."

"I don't understand. Did they say why?"

He told her about the visit from the board member and how the conversation spun out of control.

"I really wanted to hit him," Ford said.

"I'm glad you didn't. I'm so sorry. This is all because of me. Is there anything I can do? I could get my lawyer to write a threatening letter."

"Thank you. I might take you up on the offer, but I have a lot to think about. The school goes on break in a couple of days. It might make sense to take the next couple of weeks, get through the holidays, and then decide the best way to handle this mess."

"Are you sure you don't want to act now? Why wait?"

"Because I'll be impulsive in my actions. Just like kissing you in front of all those people. I knew you were being watched, but I didn't give a damn. I should have. I should have known better. I'm a damn high school principal."

"You're a man. A very sexy man whom I wanted to kiss too." She placed a hand on his cheek because she had to touch him.

He removed her hand from his cheek. "Nyx, now isn't the time."

She scooted back in the seat. "So you just wanted to hunt me down so you could what... blame me? Yell at me? Why are you here, Ford?"

"I needed to see you. My feelings for you are the only thing that makes sense. When I'm with you, I'm happy. But this week, I was angry at first at you, then at myself."

"It's going to be okay. Let me make a few calls for you."

"Please don't. I can't have you fixing my problems for me."

"If you change your mind, let me know. Can I kiss you now?"

He choked out a laugh.

Her phone vibrated in her pocket. She pulled it out to read Miles' name. "I can ignore that."

"It's okay. Really. See what he wants. It might be

important. I'll drive you home and we can make out in the driveway like when we were kids."

"Sounds good to me." She swiped the screen. "Hello, Miles."

"Nyx, I thought I was going to get your voicemail. Glad I caught you. What the hell were you thinking giving those people the bird?"

"It was an impulse."

"Of course, it was. Typical Nyx. Look your little stunt paid off. I've got venues calling me left and right to see if you'll come play at their space. Most of them are small, not what we're used to, but it's a good way to get you back out there. We'll work our way up to the big arenas again."

"What's this *we* stuff?"

"You need a manager. You're not handling this incident as the opportunity it is. Your assistant told me you're ignoring the interview requests too. Let me run with this. There's a venue right in New Jersey, that godawful state of yours, and they want you tomorrow night."

"Tomorrow night?"

"Are you having trouble hearing me? Do you want me to text?"

"I can hear you fine." Well, enough anyway which she wouldn't tell Miles. She wasn't sure if she was ready to get back on stage in front of an audience. What if the same thing happened? She had expected to be better by now.

"What do you say? Can I call them and say you'll be there?"

"I haven't played in over a month. I'd need to practice." She couldn't just jump on stage cold. That could be a disaster.

"You can rehearse before the show. You're a pro and so is your band."

"I don't know that you should be my manager with all our history." Miles was very good at his job. She had to give him that much. He wouldn't risk another embarrassing situation to his career and suggest she perform, if he didn't think she could. Maybe this could work out.

Ford stole a glance at her and raised a brow. She gave him the one-minute sign in return.

"This is business. I can put the past aside if you can. I'm the best at what I do and you have moved on to a new guy from what it looks like. No use crying over spilled beer and all that."

He didn't seem too upset by her kissing Ford. More like spurred on by the chance to make a comeback. Miles was consistent and always upfront about who he was. She should not be surprised by this call or his reaction to her.

"Will you do it?" he said.

"I need to talk to Luther about the sound system." She had to ask him if there was a way he could arrange the speakers and the cabinets to help her hear the music better.

"He'll be there. I will escort him myself. *Will you do it?*" Miles' enthusiasm was palpable.

She stole a glance at Ford as he pulled into her driveway. She had an idea. "I'll do it if you let me bring a new guitar guy. I've been working with him, and he's the best."

"Is that it?"

"That's it."

"Done. I'll text you the address and the times. Bring your guy. Oliver is playing with another band anyway. This is going to be great, Nyx. Welcome back." He ended the call.

Was she back if her hearing wasn't one hundred percent yet?

"Who is this new guitar guy? You never mentioned anyone." Ford unhooked his seat belt and faced her.

She grabbed his hand. "Miles has an opportunity for me to play tomorrow night right here in Jersey. I'm going to take it and smooth out some of the mess I've made recently. Will you come with me?"

"Sure. My mom will watch Delaney. I'd be happy to be your moral support." His smile ignited those sexy creases around his eyes.

"That's not what I mean." Excitement bubbled in her belly. She could picture him on stage beside her, strumming the guitar.

"You don't want moral support?"

"I want you to play with me. You're the new guitar guy." She almost jumped out of her seat with the thrill of this new plan. They would be able to jam together for the first time in ages. As they should have been all along. He didn't know the music, but they would figure something out. She could text Miles and say her new guy was more rhythm instead of lead. She wasn't worried.

"Me?" He pulled away. "I can't play with you. That's crazy. I told you what happened when I went on stage the other night. No way. I'll go to stand by your side. That's it."

"Come on, please. You were drunk the last time. This will be different. You'll be great. I know it."

"I don't know your music. I can't get on stage and play. I haven't even practiced. I've had enough embarrassing experiences these past weeks to last me a lifetime. No, thanks."

"I don't care whether or not you know the music well. Take a chance. Do it. Jump." Her insides vibrated. She wanted him to feel the excitement that she did. He could finally let go and be the person he had always wanted to be.

"At the risk of ruining your night? Please don't put that kind of pressure on me." He hopped out of the car. She followed.

"Ford, I'm handing you an opportunity. Run with it."

"I can't. Thank you for having faith in me even after all this time and especially after this past week, but I won't embarrass you that way."

She came around the car and put her hands on his chest. "Please."

"I think it's best if I decline."

"I understand. You don't want to do it." Her heart sunk, but she tried to shake it off. "Will you come anyway?" She needed him there to be her rock in case she ruined her own night.

He placed a kiss on her lips. "As long as I don't have to get on stage to perform, I will gladly be by your side, if you think you're ready. Are you? Is the hearing better?"

"It's fine." If she said it enough times, maybe it would be true.

CHAPTER TWENTY-FOUR

Nyx stood over the toilet and threw up—again. The tinnitus screamed in her head. Her stomach convulsed. She stood and wiped the sweat from her brow.

She couldn't go on stage. Her legs could barely carry her out of the ladies' room at the White Rock Music Hall. Her nerves and the vertigo had the best of her. The ringing in her ears had grown progressively worse as the day wore on. When Ford had picked her up, she could barely hear a word he said.

She couldn't wear her hearing aids on stage. The sound would be unbearable. She had to go on without anything to help lower the tinnitus.

"Nyx." Ford banged on the stall door. "Are you okay?"

She flung open the door and threw herself in his arms. He held her close and ran a hand over the back of her head. "It won't stop. I don't know what to do."

He eased out of the embrace and looked at her. "Is there any way you can sing?"

"No way. Not with the music playing."

"Then you don't go on."

"I can't cancel again. I have to fix this."

"You can't fix it. You have to accept it."

"No."

Miles barged into the bathroom with Luther on his heels. "What the hell, Nyx? You should've been on twenty minutes ago."

Ford stepped in front of her. "She's sick."

"She was fine while they practiced," Miles said.

"She's not fine now." Ford puffed up his chest and stood his full height.

"I don't care if she needs an appendectomy. You're getting on that stage." Miles peered around Ford and pointed at her.

"Back up or I will back you up." Ford stepped into Miles' personal space. Miles bumped into Luther.

Luther gave Nyx a kind smile. "Any chance you can try, Nyx? I'll be in the front of the house with my boards. I won't let anything happen to you. I'll keep the volume as low as I can. I even miked the cabinet."

She wanted to say she would do it. She wanted to be brave and push through this, but the motor wouldn't stop. Once the guitar and drums kicked in, the pain would sear through her head. She wouldn't be able to hear herself if her life depended on it.

"I can't."

"You're finished. You hear me? You're a loser. No one will ever work with you again. I will see to it." Miles lunged toward her.

She jumped back into the stall door. Ford stepped forward and shoved Miles into the sink. Miles let out an "Oof" and crumpled to the floor. Luther stared between the two men.

"I'll be outside," Luther said and went through the door.

"Talk to her like that again and I'll hand you your teeth. You hear me now?"

She placed a hand on his arm. He stiffened. "Ford, it's okay."

Miles climbed to his feet. "Tough guy, can you sing? You want to go on?"

"Yes, that's a great idea." Why hadn't she thought of that herself? They could save a little face by providing someone to sing.

"I can't go out there."

She cupped his face in her hands. "You can do this. You know plenty of music. You sing with Delaney all the time. It doesn't have to be my music."

"This isn't my dream anymore. You're my dream." He gripped her hands and held them by his chest.

She pulled away, disgusted by the whole night. "Why do you want me? Look at me, vomiting in the bathroom. He's right." She pointed at Miles. "I have nothing to offer you. Forget about me."

She ran from the bathroom before he could say another thing. She ran until her legs gave up, her lungs burned, and the area around her was as unrecognizable as her life had become.

She pulled her phone out of her back pocket and sent a text to Petra, asking her to come and pick her up.

It would be an hour before Petra could get to her.

She found an ice cream store and sat at a metal table outside the shop to wait. Ford tried to reach her several times, but she ignored the texts and let the calls go to voicemail.

She had nothing to say. She had nothing to give. Nothing would be right again.

Her hearing would never go back to normal.

And neither would she.

He was through with Nyx. Ford pulled into his driveway and dragged himself out of the car. The cold night air bit into his skin. He was thankful he could still feel something. After the past two days, he wasn't sure he had anything left inside him.

He let himself into the house. His mother was asleep on the couch. She had agreed to come over and watch Delaney at his house for a change. Tonight, he wished she had taken Delaney to her place. Delaney would demand his attention first thing and he didn't have the energy left to care for another human being.

He had no idea what Nyx wanted from him. She had jumped into his arms for support, then pushed him to get on stage when he didn't want to, only to go running out into the night like a banshee. She hadn't answered a single text or call. What if she were dead in a ditch? The least she could do was tell him she was okay.

He ran a hand over his face. If he knew Nyx, she had hitchhiked to Nashville by now, leaving him and Delaney behind. She had said no promises. He wished he had listened.

He dumped his coat on the kitchen chair and kicked his shoes off where he stood. Tomorrow he could clean it all up.

"How was your evening?" His mother stood in the doorway. She shoved a hand in her hair and her face was void of makeup. Golda was still beautiful at her age. His mother had always been there for him. She had silently told him to go for his dreams all those years ago, but it had been his father's blessing he craved. If his father had said one word to him that he understood what Ford needed, he would have run to Nyx.

"A nightmare."

"What happened?"

"I don't want to talk about it." He looked inside the fridge for a beer and found none.

"I can make some tea." She came into the kitchen and patted him on the shoulder. Before he could stop her, she filled the teakettle with water and put it on the stove.

"I still don't want to talk about it."

"She couldn't do it, could she?" Golda pulled two tea bags out of the box.

"Mom, please. Not now. It's been a hell of a night. I'm going to bed."

She gripped his arm. "Ford, I love you more than anything in this world. But you need to get your head out of your backside. This time isn't like when you were kids. She would give up her hearing for good if it meant she could sing one more time the way it was before."

"How do you know this? Are you a mind reader now?"

"I'm a mother, dear. A mother knows even when it's not her child. And Nyx was like a daughter to me. Go be

254

her rock. Stand beside her no matter what craziness possesses her now."

"She doesn't want me. She said as much."

"She's afraid."

"Nyx?" He had never known Nyx to be afraid of anything. But she had been sad this time around. Her eyes had given her away more than once.

"Yes, even Nyx."

"I'll think about it." After he got some sleep.

"For once, think with your heart."

CHAPTER TWENTY-FIVE

"Daddy, I won't do the show without Nyx." Delaney stood in the kitchen in her green stocking feet and her hands on her hips. Her Christmas bow was crooked again.

This conversation had taken up the better part of the last hour. Today was Christmas Eve and the showcase at the winery. He hadn't spoken to Nyx since the White Rock Music Hall. Every time he grabbed the phone to text or call, he couldn't do it. She had run away from him, leaving him with Miles. Ford understood that she had been upset, devastated even, but she continued to ignore him. His mother might be right about Nyx, but they couldn't be in a relationship, if at the end of the day she didn't trust him to be there for her.

"Delaney, you're doing the show. You've practiced. You have a time slot set up. The people who put on the showcase are counting on you. We follow through on our obligations."

"I can't sing if she isn't there."

"You're going to have to." If he had to carry her and deposit her on the stage, he would. She had begged him to do this thing until he had caved, and he had been against it.

"Why can't you get Nyx to come? I thought she liked us." Delaney's face scrunched up and turned red. Tears poured down her cheeks. "Does she think I'm weird like the kids at school?"

He dropped down to his knee and pulled her into a hug. "Nyx likes you very much. She thinks you're cool and funny and loves your bows. It's me she's mad at. Remember I told you that Nyx might not feel well enough to help with the showcase?"

"Yes." Delaney hiccupped and wiped her nose with the back of her hand.

"She's not feeling great right now. We need to give her a little space to feel better."

"No, Daddy. When someone doesn't feel well, we have to make them feel better. She needs a favorite blanket and comfy pajamas." She sniffled again.

"It's a little different kind of sick." He handed her a napkin, and she wiped her nose.

"Can we go and visit her?"

"I'm afraid not." She did not want to see him. She had made that abundantly clear when all he wanted to do was protect her.

"You have to go make her feel better. Please, Daddy. I can't sing without her. She's like a good luck charm."

He bit back a laugh because Delaney was serious. She placed her hands on his shoulders and gave a shove. "Go, Daddy."

"Okay. I'll try one more time. For you." He couldn't

tell his child no and as far as Nyx was concerned, she owed Delaney her presence at the show.

Delaney planted a wet kiss on his cheek. "It's the only thing I want for Christmas."

Too bad he didn't know that before he had bought all those presents. "I'll be back soon. Stay with Lolli. She needs the company. She's old."

"I heard that," his mother said from the living room.

Ford hurried to Nyx's house. He hoped she was there and knocked on the door. The lock clicked and the door opened. Huck stood there with a death stare in his blue eyes and a snarl on his lip. His red sweater pulled across his chest.

"What are you doing here?" Huck's glare bore through him.

"I came to talk to Nyx. Is she home?" He refused to squirm under this man's scrutiny. He wouldn't leave until Nyx came to the door.

"Is she expecting you?"

"No. But it's important. It's about the showcase and my daughter. Could you please tell her I'm here?"

"What are your intentions with my daughter, young man?" Huck crossed his arms over his chest.

"Sir, your daughter has a mind of her own. I'm sure I don't have to tell you that, but my intentions, though honorable, don't matter a hill of beans since she's not buying."

Huck burst out laughing and slapped his leg. "As long as you understand she's always in the driver's seat, you'll be all right. Going to take a strong, sensible man with a whole lot of patience to be with my Nicole."

He didn't think he was the guy for the job anymore. "I hope she finds him."

Huck waved his hand through the air. "Ah. You young folk today. Think you know everything when the obvious stuff sits there ready to bite you in the bottom. Stay put. I'll get her." He started to close the door and yelled for Nyx.

Ford paced the porch. They had a few hours before they needed to be at the winery. He hoped she didn't make him wait out here until the last minute. He was about to give up when the door opened.

Nyx stepped outside in an oversized flannel shirt and black leggings. She pulled her hair over her ears and he had to wonder if she put on her hearing aids today. All he wanted to do was pull her into his arms and tell her everything would be okay. Whatever her hearing turned out to be, he didn't care. He didn't give a damn if she ever stepped onto a stage again unless that was what she wanted. He would help her find the best solution to her problem, but at some point, that stubborn woman needed to accept her reality.

"Hey," he said.

"Hey. What's up?" She pulled the shirtsleeves down over her hands.

"Will you be at the showcase today?" The space between them killed him. He wasn't sure how he was going to continue his life without her as a part of it.

"No."

"Delaney won't sing without you there."

She flinched. At least he hit a nerve.

"She doesn't need me."

"Tell that to the nine-year-old. You promised her. I

warned you about this. I'm only asking one more thing of you for Delaney's sake. Do the right thing for her, please."

"My tinnitus is bad today. I won't be able to sit through the show. Tell her I'm proud of her and she's going to be great." Tears filled her eyes.

He took a step forward. She took a step back. His heart fell to his shoes.

"Nicole, don't shut me out. You don't have to do this alone."

"I'm no good for you. I'm the one who ruined your career, as well as my own. I just wanted my hearing to go back to the way it was so I could have my career. And I wanted you to go for your dreams."

"Dreams change. Yours can too. You can have music in your life another way."

"What are you going to do about the superintendent position?"

"I don't know. Right now, I have a child at home who teeters between temper tantrums and joy. I need her to go to that showcase so she can prove to herself she can do it. That's more important than my job." He didn't even want to think about the dead end his career had hit. There was no time for it.

"You weren't saying that you wanted her to sing when the lessons started."

"Dreams aren't the only thing that change. I was wrong about that. She needs this for her self-confidence. She needs you there for that too."

"She doesn't need me. She needs to see her dad going for the things that matter to him the most. She shouldn't have to watch you waste away in a career you don't really love."

"The thing that matters to me most is standing in front of me. You refuse to follow what's in your heart, not me. We love each other. Don't bother denying it. But you'd rather chase the only thing you can't have because you think it's what makes you a whole person. It doesn't."

"I can't hear right." She slapped her legs with her hands.

"Then read my lips. I don't give a damn if you can hear the way you used to. I don't care if you have a giant music career or you're a music teacher. I love you exactly the way you are. You need to start loving yourself that way too."

He brushed past her and slid into the car. He drove away without looking back for fear he would crumble under the hurt.

Nyx stood on the porch as Ford sped out of the driveway. His tires screeched on the road when he drove away. She heard that and almost smiled. Her hearing was pretty good today. She had lied about the tinnitus. Facing a crowd of people, sitting through the entire showcase, was more than she could handle. Too many people would have questions about her career and the recent viral videos. Now she couldn't even say she and Ford were together. They were better apart.

The door opened and her father stepped out on the

porch. "Your man left already? He isn't staying for Christmas Eve dinner?"

"He's not my man."

"Does he know that? Because he's in love with you."

"How can you tell?" She never took her father for an expert on relationships.

"I was his age once. I know that look he has in his eye."

"Ugh, Dad. Spare me. I'm going inside."

"Hang on a second." He put his hand up. "Is he right?"

"About what?" She did not want to have this conversation with her father. She wanted to go back in the house and sit in front of the television, watching corny Christmas movies until her teeth hurt.

"About you not accepting yourself."

"No… I don't know." She dropped onto the porch swing. Her dad sat next to her. The swing creaked under his weight.

"This thing with your hearing isn't fair. Life rarely is. SJ being murdered in a back alley wasn't fair either. Silas having to raise his babies alone wasn't fair. Kind of like your Ford has to do with his girl. He has it hard too."

"I'm not trying to minimize what he goes through as a single parent. I had a plan for myself. I was supposed to get my hearing back."

"The doctors said that's not possible."

"I still tried." Maybe she had been foolish to think she could come up with a solution by herself.

"Nothing wrong with trying. Accepting is another thing."

"You're starting to sound like Ford."

"Maybe he's not so bad after all. I have a Christmas present for you. Wait here a minute." Her father pushed off the swing and went inside.

She had a few presents for Ford and Delaney, but she didn't know how to get them over to Ford's now. Maybe Petra or Ember would drop them off or she could leave them with Golda if she wasn't furious with Nyx too.

Huck returned a few minutes later with a small rectangular package wrapped in Santa paper and handed it to her. "Opening one on Christmas Eve was your momma's favorite thing."

"Yeah. She loved to sit and watch us all, never opening one for herself." Her mother would sit on the floor with her legs tucked under her as they tore through the one present they could have before morning.

"Go on, now. See what it is." He sat back down and tapped her knee.

She lifted the corners of the wrinkled paper and the tape gave way under her touch. She pulled out a book about tinnitus.

"Now, don't get mad at me because I gave you a book about your problem. This here has a method that might help you live with it. Can't make it go away, but it can make it take a back seat of sorts. Read it. It helped a lot of people like you."

"How did you find this?" She turned the book over in her hand. He had given her a book about meditation and rewiring her brain.

"On one of those podcast things."

"You know what a podcast is?"

"Sure. Paige showed me. Now go clean up and get to that showcase. You're a Wilde. We don't let down the people we love. Your man and his little girl need you." He stood again.

"He's pretty mad at me."

Huck waved his hand through the air. "Ah. Your mother was mad at me plenty of times in our lives. Never stopped loving me though. Not once. Real love sticks. I got to get inside and finish that ham. Silas and his bunch will be here right after the show ends. Hurry now."

"Dad?"

He turned back.

"Thank you. I love the book… and you."

"Ah."

CHAPTER TWENTY-SIX

Ford could not believe he was doing this. He had already embarrassed himself plenty these last few weeks. What was one more time, even if it was in front of the entire town and then some?

He and Delaney waited in the wings of the makeshift stage at the River Winery. His guitar was tuned and ready to go. More so than he was. They would be singing a Christmas tune. He shouldn't be nervous, but his nerves ate away at his insides. He hadn't known the one Delaney and Nyx had practiced and had no time to learn it. Delaney was okay with the song change because they had sung it for years while decorating their Christmas tree.

The audience was packed with more people he knew than he didn't. His mother and father sat in the front row. His mother chatted with Clarence Chambers, Lyra's mother, while his father sat forward with his lips puckered.

Delaney bounced on her toes next to him. She had

decided to wear her red Christmas dress with the white feathery collar and hem. She looked like a full-size Santa hat. Her bow was red and white to match. She had only agreed to perform tonight if he sang with her. He couldn't say no after Nyx had. He would do anything for his little girl, including humiliating himself in front of everyone. Yeah, he was going to throw up.

People scurried by backstage. Weezer River shouted orders to the stage crew and volunteers. Rumors had flown around about her here tonight, but Ford was too busy calming his anxiety to pay much attention. He did notice a ballerina, as did Delaney. She wanted to try dancing next.

He peeked out from the side of the curtain again. Most of Nyx's family took up an entire row—her father as well as her two sisters and their husbands or fiancés or whatever they were. Her niece Paige was there, pointing her phone up at the stage. Ford also noticed her cousins Brad, with Lyra Chambers, and Brooklyn, who bounced her little girl on her lap, and Brooklyn's husband Caleb.

He was definitely going to be sick.

"You're up next," Malbec River said and hurried off to help a woman stuck inside a Christmas box prop.

"Daddy, this is going to be fun." Delaney tugged on his arm, knocking his guitar.

"Sure is." Or he would pass out on stage. But in a few minutes the torture would be over.

"Do you have room for one more?" Nyx appeared at his side with a wide smile and a twinkle in her eye.

"Nyx." Delaney jumped into Nyx's arms. "You came. Do you feel better?"

Nyx readjusted Delaney's bow that slid to the side of her head. "I feel a lot better now. I'm sorry I'm late."

"It's fine. Daddy is going to sing too. Now all three of us can."

"This is a chance for you and your dad to sing together. I only came to wish you luck and applaud you when you're done."

"Please sing with us," Delaney said.

Nyx held his gaze. "It's up to you."

"Will you be okay out there?" He didn't want her to do anything that made her uncomfortable.

"If we sing a cappella. Can we do that?"

"What's that?" Delaney said.

He removed his guitar and placed it to the side. "We sing without instruments so Nyx can hear us."

She pulled back her hair. "I only wore one. Let's see how it goes. I'll pull it out if it doesn't work. Ford, I'm sorry about what I said to you. It's your life. I support whatever you want to do."

"You were right. I do want to do this kind of thing more. Dip my toes in a little, but I'm scared to death." Hell, he didn't know if he could sing a two-minute Christmas song.

"Me too." She laced her hand through his.

"I'm sorry I didn't realize how frightened you were before now. I didn't mean to push you away from your dreams. I just wanted you to know I wasn't judging you," he said.

"I've been judging myself too hard and like you said, dreams change. I'm taking a detour for now. Will you come with me?" She stepped closer.

"Where are you going?"

"I'm staying right here for now. Where you and Delaney are." Nyx looked between him and Delaney, then gave Delaney's nose a little squeeze. Delaney giggled.

"Are you saying you're going to stay?"

"I am. I want us to have a real chance this time if you don't mind putting up with me while I learn how to deal with my hearing in a more productive way."

"I'm here for whatever you need. For the first time in a long time, I don't care about the unknown. With you beside me, I can trust myself and let go a little."

"I promise to trust that you know what you want for yourself. You don't need me to force you into anything."

"Keep pushing me. Please." He placed a kiss on her lips.

"So... what song are we singing?" Nyx clapped her hands and glanced at Delaney.

"We're going with a different Christmas song because Dad wasn't prepared for the one we've been practicing. Is that okay?"

"I can do that. Which one?"

"'Every Christmas Without You,'" he said.

"That song I wrote when I first started out? On that awful Christmas album the label made me do?" A laugh burst from her lips.

"It's our favorite Christmas song," Ford said. "We sing it every year."

Nyx's eyes filled with tears.

"Ladies and gentlemen, let's give a big round of applause for our next act. Ford and Delaney McKay singing a Christmas tune," said the show's host.

The audience burst into applause.

"Go," Weezer yelled.

He took his daughter's hand in one and Nyx's in the other and together they walked out onto the stage.

Nyx held tight to Ford's hand. As long as he was by her side, she would weather whatever came her way. And if she lost her hearing completely, he would be the anchor to hold her safe and sound. Just like he had been all along. But maybe this time, he would fly a little with her, because she had a lot more living to do and she wanted to start right now.

The stage lights blurred some of her view, but she could make out her sisters and her father in the audience. They waved, and she waved back. Love was the most important thing. More important than a stage and an audience singing along. Ford and her father had taught her that. Funny how life worked.

Ford started them off. His voice was deep and crisp. His nervous smile ignited the crinkles around his eyes and she fell in love all over again. She and Delaney joined in as if they had rehearsed this song a million times. The words and the sounds came effortlessly.

They ended the song on a high note. The audience cheered. Her family and Golda jumped to their feet. Delaney hopped off the stage into Golda's waiting arms.

Ford turned to her and leaned close. His lips brushed against her ear.

"We did it, and I didn't throw up," he whispered.

"You're a natural." She cupped his face to keep him close.

"I love you, and I want to take chances with you, if you'll be patient with me." He eased back and held her gaze.

"I want to hear you say you love me all the days I can. And if I can't hear you, then I know you will love me just the same whether I play music or not."

"We'll figure it all out together."

"Always and forever." Because that was the way it had been for them.

He kissed her on the stage in front of the audience.

"There are going to be pictures," she said.

"Let's really give them something to talk about." And he kissed her again.

EPILOGUE

A *ugust*

A crowd gathered on the lawn of the Pink Diamond Hotel on the unseasonably cool summer day. Many of Candlewood Falls' residents were in attendance. Golda and Grant McKay chatted with Clarisse Chambers. Weezer and Carter River held a giant pair of scissors for the ribbon cutting about to take place. Brooklyn Wilde-Ransom took photos of her father and brother. Even a few alpacas made the event.

A celebration was in order. The boutique hotel was ready for business—again. Renovations were finally completed after the fire last November. The people of Candlewood Falls milled around, enjoying the sun and the company of their neighbors. A far cry from the last time these town people gathered around this hotel.

Ford, Nyx, and Delaney sat under a big oak in the corner of the front yard out of the way of most of the guests. Delaney wore a light pink bow on her head. Nyx had helped her pick out the leopard print top and black leggings spotted with leopard print hearts. The pink bow matched the pink jacket and pink sneakers.

Nyx was dressed much the same way — sans the bow. Ford pulled her close.

"How long do we have to stay?" Ford asked.

"Long enough to see my uncle happy. Like us." She snuggled against him.

"He looks pretty happy to me." Ford glanced over at Silas, lifting Claudia into the air and spinning her around. Many people broke out into applause.

"I also want some time with my adorable new nephew." Ember and her husband Raf sat nearby fussing over their infant son. Raf had married Ember on the way to the delivery room only hours before Nicolas came screaming into the world. Ember had decided she didn't want to have the baby after they were married as originally planned. Unfortunately, she had forgotten to tell Raf in enough time to plan anything more than a dash down the hospital hallway.

"What do you think about us making a baby?" Ford whispered in her ear.

"Right here in the yard?"

"Funny lady. Before I go on tour. I can't believe I'm evening saying those words."

Nyx had made a few calls after the holidays and found a gig for Ford, playing on a colleague's album who was down a guy. Colton Savage loved Ford's bass guitar playing so much, Colton asked Ford to join him and his brother on tour at the end of summer.

"Let's at least practice before you leave." For Nyx, the limelight would wait. She was busy writing songs other people would sing, and she was good with that for now because she had what she truly wanted right in front of her.

The rest would work itself out. In the meantime, her tinnitus gave her a much-needed reprieve from time to time thanks to the book her father bought her last Christmas. Not all days were good, but some were great.

"Can we go then?" Ford climbed to stand and held out his hand.

"Soon. Delaney, do you want to visit with little Nicolas for a bit?" She stood and took Ford's hand.

"Yes. Yes." Delaney jumped up and down.

"Run over to Miss Ember and make sure to give Mr. Huck a big hug. I'll be along in a second, okay?"

"Miss Ember,…" Delaney ran to where Ember sat with Raf, Petra, Mav, and Huck. Delaney threw her arms around Huck's neck, and he bellowed with laughter.

"I can drop Delaney at my parents' house later so we can have a little alone time." Ford kissed her cheek.

"That would be nice." Nyx took in the scene before her. "You know, Candlewood Falls is filled with people who show up when the chips are down, no questions asked. Like they did for Silas and Claudia."

"That's the thing about small towns. The people who live in them will open their arms and welcome you in," Ford said.

"Or push you out." Nyx thought about Ford's super-intendent application being denied.

He laughed. "Yeah, that too. But all we have to do is look around us at your family and mine to see the real meaning of caring and love."

Nyx placed a kiss on Ford's lips then held his gaze.

"All I have to do is look at you."

ALSO BY STACEY WILK

Serenity Series

Sea Glass Made with Second Chances

Sea Glass Hidden in Plain Sight

Sea Glass Out of Balance

Sea Glass Wrapped in Red

Heritage River Series

The Risk for House and Home

The Bridge Between Love and Lies

The Essence of Whiskey and Tea

Hometown Series

Taking Root

Raising Winter

Defining Chances

Beginning Over

Steeling Hearts

Whispering Christmas

Winter at the Shore Series

No More Darkness

Through the Darkness

Light Upon the Darkness

The Brotherhood Protectors World

Winter's Last Chance

The Last Betrayal

Her Last Word

The Last Days of Christmas

Seduced by Denial

Chill in the Air

Fighting for Tessa

Nash's Promise

Cruz's Watch

Harlan Unleashed

<u>Big Sky Country Series</u>

Time Won't Erase

Stay Awhile

Love Never Ends

Dare to Tell (coming soon)

READY FOR ANOTHER TRIP TO
CANDLEWOOD FALLS?

Be sure to check out these other 2023 Christmas books in the Candlewood Falls world.

Wilde Under the Mistletoe by K.M. Fawcett

A Little Bit Whiskey by Jen Talty

ACKNOWLEDGMENTS

Let me start by saying, I had to do a lot of research to understand Nyx's hearing problems and do justice to her story and anyone who may have a similar path to walk. I read several books on tinnitus and hearing loss. I watched and listened to many interviews with musicians who suffer from this problem.

But I need to give a special thanks to Jen Talty who graciously shared her own experience with tinnitus and put up with my countless questions. Any and all mistakes are mine, for which I apologize. If I took any creative liberties for the sake of the story, I hope you'll understand.

I need to thank my content editor, Robin Rottner, for incredible feedback on this book and all my other ones. She asks the best questions!

I need to beat the drum for Jen and Kathy who took this ride with me through six books. Thank you, ladies. It's been fun.

And always I must say thank you to my constant readers. Thank you for showing up again and again, allowing me to entertain you with my stories and for spending time in Candlewood Falls. I hope you enjoyed your visit.

A special shout out to Stacey's B*tches for all your love and making me laugh every Wednesday night. You ladies rock and roll.

ABOUT THE AUTHOR

From an early age, best-selling and award-winning author, Stacey Wilk, told tales as a way to escape. At six she wrote short stories in composition notebooks, at twelve she wrote a novel on a typewriter, in high school biology she wrote rock star romances in her binder instead of paying attention.

But it wasn't until many years later, inspired by her children and a looming birthday, that she finally took her story-telling seriously. And published her first novel in 2013. Since then, she's gone on to publish thirty-one more so women everywhere can indulge in books that hook them heart and soul.

She isn't done telling stories. Not by a long shot. If you want to read her emotional and honest books about family, romance, and second chances, visit her at www.staceywilk.com

To see what she writes next, follow her Facebook group for her amazing readers – Stacey's Novel Family https://bit.ly/2FK8Lae

Or join her newsletter - https://bit.ly/2A0jEFk